The Tortoise Cried its Only Tear

The Tortoise Cried its Only Tear

CAROL CAMPBELL

UMUZI

Published in 2019 by Umuzi,
an imprint of Penguin Random House South Africa (Pty) Ltd
Company Reg No 1953/000441/07
The Estuaries No 4, Oxbow Crescent, Century Avenue,
Century City, 7441, South Africa
PO Box 1144, Cape Town, 8000, South Africa
umuzi@penguinrandomhouse.co.za
www.penguinrandomhouse.co.za

First edition, first printing 2019
1 3 5 7 9 8 6 4 2

ISBN 978-1-4152-1008-6 (Print)
ISBN 978-1-4152-1034-5 (ePub)

Cover design by Monique Cleghorn
Cover photography from iStock.com/mustafa6noz
Text design by Chérie Collins
Set in 11 on 14 pt Adobe Caslon Pro
Printed and bound by Novus Print, a Novus Holdings company

MIX
Paper from
responsible sources
FSC
www.fsc.org   FSC® C022948

For Stuart and David

Chapter 1

NOW

Siena knew she was on the Sand River road. Behind her was the town, and far ahead lay Seekoegat and her old primary school, which was on the tar road to Beaufort West. From town to Seekoegat was three days on the donkey karretjie, but that was with stops. When she was a child, and Pa was still spanning fences, they had lived on many of the farms between here and Seekoegat. Those were in the days when they had the cart and the boere didn't mind the donkeys coming in for water. When it rained, Pa had steered the cart towards the Gamka or Swart River so that he could ask for work from the sheep farmers. When those rivers came down, which was maybe once a year, they took with them all the river mats, and then there was plenty for a draadmaker to do. Those were the best times for them on the karretjie – when the rivers came down.

Siena's heart was pounding, and she was breathing hard from running.

'Oh, dear God … oh, God.' She stopped, put her hands on her knees, and looked back at the lights of the town. 'Oh, God, they are coming.'

And she started to run again. It must have been close to midnight, because the moon was high in the black Karoo sky. Despite the hour, Siena could make out the Swartberg, and she wondered if it would be better to cross the veld and head into the mountains.

'No, no,' she said aloud.

Aunt Esme and Meneer Maans at Seekoegat Primary would know what to do. Her hands and arms were sticky from blood. She wiped them on her pants but it didn't help. Dry blood on her shirt and face made her look as if she had been attacked and, if she could have seen herself, she knew she would have cried out in fright. She had to keep running; then everything would be okay.

Even now, after the terrible thing she had done, her mind wandered, and she thought about Pa and those times when she was very small and they had lived on the karretjie. And then that one year, after the Gamka, he'd insisted they trek into the valley because the river there would have flooded too and there would be work. It was in the valley when everything changed. Siena remembered how they had waited three days for the mevrou so Pa could speak to her. And, when he'd come back to the karretjie, he was happy. This was a long-time job, he'd said.

It was in the valley that Siena had met Boetie. That man, Majola, had told Pa to outspan close to where he lived with Ou Ana and Boetie. Ma had wanted him to ask if they could stay on the mevrou's place, but Pa had said he knew Majola from long ago and it would be good to have someone he knew to talk to around the fire at night. And Ou Ana would talk to Ma like she was a person, not like the town women who blocked their noses with their fingers when she came close. It was in the valley that Pa had sold the donkeys, Pienkie and Haas. One of the kleinboere had given him two hundred rand for the cart with the donkeys. Ma had said they needed the money for flour and, anyway, she was sick and tired of chasing after donkeys. Later on, Pa heard the donkeys had been shot.

The man who had bought them said they'd cost too much to feed and he got more than his two hundred rand back when he'd sold the meat. Siena knew that Pa had been sad because he had taught those donkeys to plough and it was hard to find donkeys that knew how to do that. For many weeks afterwards, he had told her stories about how Pienkie and Haas could plough: 'If I shouted *links, links, links*, then they would go left, and if I shouted *regs, regs, regs*, they would go right.' Pa would hold his hands up as if he had the reins and he was guiding them across a field. 'It was very hard to teach stubborn donkeys to listen like that,' he said. 'I shouldn't have sold them. That man should never have shot good donkeys that knew how to plough.'

It was when Pa was working in the valley that Siena had been sent away to Seekoegat Primary School. The mevrou had taken her in the big white farm bakkie and left her at the school with a plastic packet from Pep with grey pants and a white shirt, and told her she was there to learn how to behave. Many times after that, Siena had smiled and then cried when she remembered that time and what the mevrou had said. She had been so afraid and, when the mevrou had driven away from the school, Siena'd thought she would run away all the way back to Ma and Pa. She had been thinking about doing that on her very first day at Seekoegat Primary, when Aunt Esme had spied her and called her to the door of the school's kitchen.

'What's your name, Klimmie?'

'Siena.'

She spoke so softly, Aunt Esme had shouted like the ou was deaf: 'Say again?' And she'd tilted her head towards Siena to hear.

'Siena,' she'd whispered.

'Where do you come from?'

Siena had looked at her feet and said nothing. This aunt

spoke so loudly, it made Siena want to pee from being scared.

Aunt Esme raised her eyebrows. 'Not a talker, hey? Well, better than one who talks too much. Why are you so filthy? You stink, jong.'

Keeping her head down and her eyes on her dusty toes, Siena had lifted the packet and given it to the aunt.

'Is this all you have? Where are your broekies and your nightdress? Did you come with a blanket?' When Siena didn't answer, Aunt Esme muttered something she couldn't hear, then said: 'Have you been to school before?'

Siena covered her face with her hands.

'Dear Jesus, another one left for us to sort out. All right, don't worry. You are going to be in grade one. You can't be a dommeid your whole life. It's good you are here, even though you are very big for grade one.'

The other children had been in class when the mevrou had arrived with Siena, but now a boy came outside holding a brass bell and he rang it and children exited the two classrooms. When they saw Siena with Aunt Esme, they ran to come and see.

'Ja, ja, you bunch of nosey parkers, back off and give Klimmie a chance. She is already afraid – she doesn't need you lot to make it worse.'

A tall girl with dancing eyes and big teeth had put her arm over Siena's shoulder. 'You can be my friend,' she'd said.

Siena had peeped through her fingers and, when the tall girl saw her, she had tickled her and Siena had laughed.

'So Klimmie here can smile.' Aunt Esme had laughed. 'Hannatjie, go fetch my atchar and a spoon, and we can have a little celebration for our new girl called Siena and, ag, Jirre, you children come on now, stand in a line. Ja, you bunch of godless good-for-nothings with no manners, wait now. Don't push like that! Ag, Jirre!'

The children had laughed and smacked their lips as she'd opened the jar and spooned out atchar onto each outstretched palm. When everyone was licking, she'd waved the spoon at Siena. 'Come, Klimmie, you will be sorry to miss out on this.'

Never in her life had Siena tasted such strange food.

'Aunt, is this Cape Town sweets?'

'No, no, no, Klimmie, this is just my treat for special occasions. You like it because your body wants salt and the oil. Don't worry, we will fatten you up here. Your ma will be happy when she sees you.'

Alone on the Sand River road, the memory of that time long ago and the aunt's bottle of atchar made Siena bring her palm to her mouth. Straight away she tasted the blood, and she spat into the soft sand on the edge of the road. It was then that she saw she was still holding the shard of broken glass and, as if it were a burning coal, she flung it into the veld where she heard it hit a rock and shatter. She went onto her knees, rubbing sand into her hands and then up her legs and arms and even into her hair to get rid of the blood. More than anything, she wanted water.

Distant headlights approached and she stumbled off the track, falling flat between rocks and keeping still the way Ma had taught her to hide. The headlights lit up the veld, but the bakkie passed without slowing. The dust it churned up made her cough and she spat again, then ran on.

The lights of the town had disappeared, and she thought she must now be well out onto the plains. They would come for her; she knew that. Someone would have seen her take the Sand River road and told the police. After a long time of running, she heard the rumbling and creaking of a windmill turning in the night breeze, and she climbed through the barbed wire, zigzagging between the bushes to the high-walled dam with the trough at its base. There were sheep resting near the water, and they leapt up as she approached, flocking and bleating. Siena had expected sheep, and ignored them, putting her mouth into their trough like an animal. She washed out her mouth to get rid of the blood taste and then she drank. Only when her thirst was gone did she put her hands in the clean cold water.

The smell of the sheep brought with it the smell of Pa's tobacco, and when she looked up he was sitting with his back against the dam wall, smoking and watching her. Pa had loved the moon and, when it was big and round and yellow like tonight, he would whip the donkeys on without stopping to make a potjie.

'A person shouldn't sleep when the moon is so beautiful,' he said now. 'Liewe Jesus has given us a big golden ball for Christmas and we need to stay awake and enjoy it.'

'It's not Christmas, Pa,' Siena said. 'Christmas is when the white people give presents and they put up decorations in OK Foods … There is nothing going on in town about Christmas.'

'Ag, Siena, Christmas is every day when it's God giving presents. Look at that big decoration in the sky and you are telling me it's not Christmas …'

He started singing then about Baby Jesus's birth, not a proper song, because he didn't know any, but his own words about donkeys and stars and the moon. When Pa finished singing, he told her a story of how his father had flown all the way to the moon and visited the animals and birds that lived there.

'Pa, people can't fly and the moon is very high in the sky. Besides, I thought it was a Christmas decoration,' she said, laughing.

'Ag, man, it's a Christmas decoration that is also a place.

'Stru, my pa knew many things about the moon that only some-one who had been there could know,' Pa said.

Siena listened to the windmill rumbling and thought about those days when she was little and they rode on the karretjie. She lay on her back with her knees bent, watching the stars. Pa lived in the stars. She knew he was there because when he was alive he used to wander into the veld and she would follow him. For a long time, he would stand alone look-ing at the sky and she knew he was talking to the people of the olden times who had died and become stars. Stars moved and talked all the time – just like people, he said. There were so many, more than all the people she had seen in her life. All the dead people from the beginning of the world were in the sky twinkling and watching what they had left behind. Now, she turned her head to watch him smoke, quiet and happy, sitting with his legs stretched and his back against the dam wall.

When she thought of Pa and all the dead people, Siena remembered what she had done, and she leapt up and howl-ed so that her voice carried across the plain like a jackal's on the night wind. The sheep, which had settled, scattered. Their sudden movement made her gasp, and she spat again. In her mind's eye, she saw the spraying blood, her baby sister's eyes, wild with fear, and her clothes covered in blood. She stumbled and fell. 'Pa, I killed him,' she wept. 'I killed a person. Pa, help me.' But, when she looked for Pa, there was no one where he had been sitting.

There had been a moment when she'd thought cutting his throat was not enough and he was going to come at her again. Even with blood spurting from the wound, he'd half-stood and turned to look at her, but his strength had failed and he'd sat down. Siena remembered that. She and Sussie had stood, pressed together against the hok wall, and watched him

13

go down. He had tried to hold himself upright with his hands gripping the table, his desperate breaths gurgling through the hole in his throat. Then his hands had loosened and he'd slid to the floor, his lips pulled back like a snarling dog, eyes glassy and staring.

The Karoo night was cool and Siena shivered. She staggered back onto her feet and ran again, the soft sand of the track giving way to the hard stony veld. But her soles were thick, and she ran with the steadiness of someone who always travelled long distances with bare feet. Even though her tears made it difficult to see, she ran on. She imagined Pa was behind her with Pienkie and Haas and that, when she grew tired, he would shout out, 'Whoa,' so she could climb onto the karretjie and catch her breath.

The pain came, first from deep within her and then to her eyes, and her mouth, which was swollen, where, earlier in the evening, he had smacked her. Black bruises rose on her arms and her ripped shirt hung off one shoulder. He had come home with the beer bottle in his hand and she'd known they'd be in for it. Straight away, Ma had slipped away like she always did, but he'd refused to let Sussie go, so she had waited in her corner, her black child-eyes afraid and unsure. Tonight, Siena had made chicken and rice and, like always, there was a plate for him. Siena had thought that would have settled things.

'Where's my dop?' he'd said.

'I didn't buy wine,' she'd lied.

'Your fokken Ma has drunk it up, nè?'

'There wasn't enough money left for wine.'

'When is there not enough money for wine in this house, you lying bitch?'

And before she could explain that she had bought Omo and sugar and candles, he'd klapped her so that she fell against the corrugated wall. The blow had stunned her, and she'd lain unmoving, eyes closed, waiting for the kicks. She should fight back. Hannatjie had once poured boiling water on her boy-friend's privates after he'd klapped her. Thinking of that, even as she'd lain on the floor, had made Siena smile, and when he saw that, he came at her so that she curled into a ball to protect herself.

'Sussie, come and sit with me,' he'd said, and Siena had heard a shuffle as the child moved from her corner.

Not Sussie.

Siena had opened her eyes as he was sliding a hand up and down Sussie's legs. He was sitting at the table again, eating with one hand, stroking Sussie with the other, and watching her.

'If you were a proper woman and not a lazy whore, we wouldn't have problems in this house,' he'd said. He put his hand behind the girl's neck and pulled her face close to his, pushing his rice-covered tongue into her mouth, so that the child whimpered. The brown glass of his broken beer bottle glinted in the candlelight and the smell of spilt beer filled the hok. As Siena had struggled to her feet, she'd picked up the big shard lying next to her.

Pa had slaughtered sheep with one swipe of his knife. 'When you kill an animal, don't mess around. If it sees what is coming, it will panic,' Pa had told her. 'And when an animal panics, its meat is tough and it doesn't die straight away. It's not nice to see.' He would hold the sheep firmly between his thighs, talking and cooing so that it stopped fighting him. And then, when its dumb sheep eyes looked into his, Pa would pick up the knife he had sharpened on a rock.

Siena had moved behind him as he ate, resting her hand on his shoulder.

Be calm, sheep.

He'd ignored her, keeping one hand on Sussie's neck and

using the other to spoon rice and chicken gravy into his mouth. When he'd sat back to chew, she had run her hand into the bush of his hair and yanked back his head. For an instant, his dead eyes had looked into hers but, before he could swing around and hit her again, she'd sliced open his throat, quick and clean, just the way Pa had shown her.

Chapter 2

BEFORE

Baas Jan hadn't come to the valley for many, many days. Boetie liked it when he stayed away because, with Baas Jan, there was always shouting. But now it had been so long that, even though Boetie hated him, he wanted him to come. He couldn't remember when the bread flour had finished and there was this problem with the water. Majola said Baas Jan knew the diesel would be finished and they couldn't pump water for the watermelons and the livestock.

'I am sure he will come today,' Majola said.

'You say that every day,' said Ou Ana, 'and then the sun comes up with no coffee and goes down with no bread.'

'I don't understand it. This man knows there is no water and still he doesn't come. His watermelons are dying and the pigs are going to start dropping one of these days. Today he must come, otherwise I am asking the mevrou to telephone his father-in-law's shop.'

During the night, Majola sent Boetie to open the gate onto the mevrou's land for the cattle to go to her dam. There would be trouble today. The mevrou didn't like Majola making these decisions without her permission, but they would have pushed over the fence anyway. Cattle didn't care about fences when they were thirsty. And anyway, Majola said to Boetie, an open gate was better than a flat fence. Boetie felt the mevrou would understand. She knew Baas Jan hadn't come, and they were feeding the pigs the watermelons and carrying water for the animals. She had started bringing down scraps mixed with mielies for the pigs and yesterday she had brought lucerne for the cattle. But water was the big problem. The sheep climbed through the fence to go to the dam, but the cattle had to go through the gate and then they plunged into the water and it was a job to get them out. The pigs were in an empty cement dam, and the only way to get them water was with a bucket or to throw them a watermelon. Baas Jan would be very angry the pigs were eating watermelons but, Boetie thought, he couldn't spend his life lugging buckets for them from mevrou's dam.

Yes, Baas Jan would come today. He had to.

Boetie wondered, if he asked Leroy's ma for a vleisie, if she would take pity on him. Last night Leroy had kaaings for supper. Boetie knew this because, when he smelt the fatty smoke, he had crept close to their fire and watched from the bushes as Leroy's ma turned the little pieces of sheep fat on the coals. When Leroy and his sister had finished eating, they'd laughed and sipped sweet coffee and wiped their greasy fingers on their arms and legs. Boetie longed for the taste of the fat and the feeling of grease running over his chin and dripping on his chest. Today he had to eat. The mevrou kept ducks in a pond on her front lawn and he thought he should steal one when she went into town. Actually, it was a good idea. The oubaas slept after lunch and Buksie, his dog, was always with him. A fat duck would surely taste very good.

When Boetie thought about food, he also thought about going to school. He knew he was old enough to go to school, and the mevrou had spoken about it to Majola. She said his big teeth were out and he wanted to be with other children and, until he went to school, the valley boys would keep him on the outside.

'You come out a dronkhuis,' Leroy said. 'Your people are godless, so you can't be our friend, and the headmaster is not going to want someone like you in our school.'

Boetie knew Majola and Ou Ana were his problem. More than anything, he wanted to go on the school bus wearing shoes. Boetie had asked Majola many times if he could go to school, but Majola always said, 'Maybe next year …' With Majola, when he didn't want to give you a straight answer, he said, 'Maybe next year …' Boetie knew that if Majola worked for the mevrou, he would have gone to school because the mevrou didn't put up with 'maybe next year'. She was kwaai about things like school. It was only because the three of them were Baas Jan's problem that nobody cared.

'Can you even write your name?' Leroy asked him, looking into his eyes and smirking as he waited for Boetie's lie.

'Ja, it's easy.'

'So write it then,' said Leroy, waiting. 'You are so stupid, you can't even write your name. Do you even know your proper name?'

Boetie could answer that one. 'I am Samuel, which is better than Leroy because Leroy sounds like a name for a baboon.' Leroy shoved him but Boetie was light and quick, and ran off laughing, scratching under his arms and making baboon noises. But he knew Leroy was right. He couldn't write his name. He wished he had a pencil so he could teach himself to write by copying from the newspaper that Majola and Ou Ana used to roll cigarettes. If boys as stupid as Leroy could learn to read and write, it couldn't be that hard.

Boetie also wasn't sure how old he was. The real valley boys knew when their birthdays were, and, on those special days, the mevrou baked a cake and the children sang 'Happy

Birthday to You'. When Boetie asked Ou Ana for his birthday, she said he must stop asking dom questions because he knew she couldn't count and Majola could only count money. Ou Ana said she couldn't remember how Boetie was born either because they had been living at the train station in those days and drinking papsak.

'All I remember is that you hung on my tiet until your teeth felt like dubbeltjies,' she said. When Ou Ana told the story – which she did often – she smacked her thighs with both hands and leant forwards, laughing as hard as she could.

'At least I have teeth,' Boetie would shoot back, 'not an empty gat like you.' Then Ou Ana would stop laughing and jump up to give him a klap, but she could never catch him, and, when he was out of her reach, he would pull his pants down and wiggle his backside.

Those conversations were all Boetie knew of his early life. He had one memory, which Ou Ana said was his mind playing tricks. He remembered clinging to a woman who was not Ou Ana one night when it was dark and very cold. They must have been lying on a road because there were screeching tyres and a flash of light. Someone rolled the woman onto her back and the voice said: 'My magtig, maar hie's 'n kind!' Then he was eating eggs in a blouhuisie and smelling coffee while the woman lay on the stoep, but, after that, the memory went as black as a night sky without stars. He was sure it happened and that someone must have found them and taken them to the house where he ate the eggs. But, he never knew who that woman was or what had happened to her.

Three nights ago, Majola had clubbed a porcupine taking bites out of the watermelons, and, once the quills were burnt off, they had roasted it over the fire. Boetie didn't tell Majola that the same day he had eaten a small tortoise. Majola was funny about eating tortoises, but Boetie didn't care. They were easy to catch and quick to cook. Besides, they all knew that when you were starving, everything could be eaten. Boetie had even braaied snakes, although he didn't think Majola and Ou Ana would have done that. If Boetie saw a snake, he killed it and cooked it. Except for a cobra – a geelslang was kwaai and stood up like a man. Nee, jinne, there were plenty of geelslang, but there was no way he was going near one, even when he was hungry. All three of them ate crabs and the bony fish Boetie caught in the mevrou's dam. They also collected eggs from muisvoël nests and ate locusts, but still they were always hungry. Every morning the three of them used Baas Jan's fencing wire to make snares which they strung along the boundary fences. If they were lucky, they caught a hare. Once, they got a duiker and, even though it was all bones, Majola gutted it and they cooked and ate it. What Boetie hated was that when the mevrou walked the fences, she took their snares down. One day she found a kudu calf dead in one of his snares, and she had her men load it on her bakkie. Leroy told him she made biltong from it and that his ma got some of the bones.

Very occasionally, if the mevrou's sheep climbed through the fence onto Baas Jan's land, Boetie and Majola cornered one and slaughtered it. Then they chased the rest of the flock up the mountainside and hid their slagding's bloody pelt in the bushes to dry. They had to be careful about cooking too much at once because Leroy's ma was always sniffing the air and, if she picked up mutton cooking that wasn't on her stove, she knew they had stolen meat. It was when their stomachs felt like this, tight and hot with hunger, that he hated Baas Jan the most. But still he wished he would come.

'You don't know how to make numbers on a telephone, so how can you call Baas Jan?' Ou Ana said to Majola. The two of them were sitting under a thorn tree near the hok smoking tobacco she had begged from Leroy's ma. Boetie was bored. He wanted to play in the dam, but the mevrou had been in a bad mood with him for the last few days and always chased him home.

'Ja, but the mevrou will know what to do. She's very clever,' said Majola.

'She likes nothing about Baas Jan. It suits her when he doesn't come.'

'Then she must feed us,' Majola said, his lips curling to show his teeth. Majola was always a happy person but Boetie knew hunger and the sukkel with the water was making him bedonnerd.

It was shop day on the farm and Boetie stood up. Maybe if he helped the mevrou with the fetching and carrying, she would give him a sweet and he would give it to Majola to put him back in a good mood. The sweet was something to look forward to. Maybe the mevrou would even give him an apple.

'Boetie, stay away from that shop,' Majola said, when Boetie stood up. 'We are beggars compared to them. Stay here and keep your pride.'

'Jinne, you can't just think my thinking like that,' said Boetie. 'My thinking is my thinking. Jissus, Majola! And anyway, shop is only in the afternoon. I am going up the koppie to watch for Baas Jan.'

Majola nodded half-heartedly. 'Stay away from that shop or I will bliksem you.'

'I won't go to the shop. Relax. If I see the green bakkie coming, I will come back.'

In a way, Baas Jan was like Majola, Boetie thought. The other farmers didn't like Baas Jan's brandy drinking and his wife was a sorry mess who walked through town with her head down to hide her bruised face. Boetie knew the look in the mevrou's eyes when she saw Baas Jan; they went small and her teeth clenched. And, of course, when Baas Jan was on the farm, the shooting started. The mevrou paced up and down her stoep, her eyes fixed on the kranse above the farmhouse as bullets smashed into the cliffs.

'Even the baboons are better than him,' Boetie had heard the mevrou tell the oubaas. 'What sort of an idiot spends the afternoon drinking brandy and shooting at the kranse?'

The oubaas had nodded. 'It's his land – there is nothing you can do.'

None of the valley farm workers would work for Baas Jan. This was because there was always a-this-way-and-a-that-way about wages. Baas Jan paid in half-packets of flour full of goggas or with vrot patats his wife couldn't sell in her father's shop. That was *when* he paid. He also bliksemed a person when he was angry. More than once, he'd knocked Majola onto his backside. When Baas Jan was in the valley, Ou Ana stayed in the bush. One time, Boetie saw him shoot a leopard that was watching them from a cave above the farm. Boetie had run to tell the mevrou, and she'd called the police, who came all the way to the valley. They took Baas Jan and his dead leopard away in their van, and that day the mevrou had given Boetie two rand for the shop.

Yes, they were happy Baas Jan didn't come too often. If only they could eat and pump water without him, then he could just stay in town. Boetie ran through the watermelon field, jumping the furrows and watching for another porcupine hiding under the big wilting leaves. When he reached the road, he crossed over into the veld, skirted the koppie, and picked his way through the rocks to the top. It was an easy climb, and when he came out at the top, he took a deep breath and sat down on his uitkyk klip. The koppie was his favourite place. In the morning, when the others were at school, he watched Leroy's ma doing her washing in a tub at her door and the oubaas on his tractor ploughing his lucerne lands. From his perch, he could see if a vehicle was approaching a long time before it arrived in the valley, which was useful when Baas Jan was expected, or if the mevrou came from town and needed help with unloading.

Today, the sky was a clean blue and two black eagles circled a field of the oubaas's new lambs. They were so close, Boetie could see the white crosses on their bellies and outstretched wings. On the opposite ridge, baboons barked, their harsh voices floating down from the cliffs. He let his eyes wander along the distant road that lay like a snake between the shimmering koppies. There was something out there today; he could feel it. He could see no dust on the valley road, so he knew it wasn't Baas Jan – maybe it was just a farm worker walking back from town. Then, carried on the breeze, he heard mevrou's old horse whinny and he knew. It was donkeys. There were donkeys coming, and when there were donkeys, there was a cart and karretjiemense. Dogs started barking and, when he focused on the far distance, he saw them – the bent shapes of a man and a woman on a donkey cart and, between them, the smaller outline of a child.

Chapter 3

At the turn-off, Jan Swart swung his bakkie onto the gravel road and headed out to his farm in the valley. He was the hell-in because the western sun was in his eyes and giving him a headache. The glare made it impossible to put his foot down, and he shifted constantly to see the road ahead. Koetie had made him late again. She knew the valley road was dead west and he had to leave before six pm to avoid the setting sun. For two weeks, he had been telling her he wanted to go to the farm, but she always said she couldn't leave her father's shop and Jan should go without her and the children. Today, when he had told her they were going, she'd done it again.

'Asseblief, Jan, my pa will hit me if he comes back and the shop is closed,' she said.

'Are you married to your pa? Hey? Hey? Hey? I am going to hit you. Maak klaar.' He raised a hand as if to slap her.

'Nee, Johan, moenie.'

'Maak klaar.'

He lunged at her, and she went onto her knees behind the till, her arms in front of her face, knowing a klap was inevitable. He laughed and kicked the counter, so that the till shuddered and the two old men waiting to pay for their tobacco moved back. They knew Baas Jan. When he was like this, it was better to be out of his way.

'Today I am not waiting for you,' he said, leaning over the counter and drumming his knuckles on her head so that she whimpered.

In his heart, Jan would have preferred his braai and brandy and Coke in the yard at the back of the shop. He didn't feel like the effort of the farm, but he wanted watermelons to sell in the lokasie; he needed the cash. Majola would think he was baas by now, and the pigs would die without water – if that idiot hadn't let them go already. Really, the responsibilities for a man were many. Koetie had no idea. She sat all day on a stool behind her father's till for sixty rand pay, and then spent the money on crayons and paper for the children if he didn't take it away from her first. No. Tonight he would make the most of it and maybe even shoot a kudu. When the kids were around, they made such a noise, the game disappeared into the mountains. Ja. Tonight, he would braai and drink and shoot and, when he came back, he would sort Koetie out once and for all so that she understood exactly who was baas. She thought her father called the shots, but Jan knew a wife belonged to the husband. Maybe if his father-in-law went to church he would know that. This had gone on for long enough. Jirre, thinking about it made him the moer-in.

There was a fifty-litre drum of diesel for the generator on the back of the bakkie which he had tied firmly with a rope. On the floor of the cab was a packet of flour and yeast that Koetie had given him for Majola, and his shotgun was propped upright against the seat. On the passenger seat, she had left wors, bread, a two-litre Coke, a twenty-pack of Stuyvesant, a box of cartridges, and a bag of his favourite sweets, the round pink-yellow apricot ones. His brandy was in a brown paper bag tucked behind the driver's seat so it wouldn't roll around and break. Ja, really. Tonight, he did not feel like having to bliksem his wife right. Tonight, he wanted to think about life and farm things – like what to plant next season, and about shooting the baboons on the ridge, and also that new girl working in the bottle store. She had given him *the* look and a very sexy smile when he'd bought his Klippies, and he knew that next weekend she would come with him to the farm if he wanted her to.

He spun the wheels of the bakkie as he accelerated away and laughed to himself when he saw the children run to get out the way. Once, when he did it, the girl had peed in her broek and he had given her a hiding for that. His boy was good, though. He got out of the way and then laughed like hell. He was good boy.

By the time Jan arrived at the turn-off, he had forgotten about them all. His pale blue eyes were screwed up from the harsh light and he was lost in thought. The road made a sharp bend and dipped through a dry riverbed where he saw kudu droppings in the sand. *They are around*, he thought. So there was a chance he would get one tonight. When the road cut between the mountain slopes, he lost the signal for Radio Sonder Grense, so he switched on the tape recorder and Steve Hofmeyr's silky voice singing 'Kyk Hoe Lyk Ons Nou' filled the cab. The tape was a compilation he had made himself by taping off the radio. He sang along and, when the song finished, he rewound the tape and played it again. He wished he had the money for a CD player but, on this road, it wouldn't have lasted anyway.

When he turned off onto the farm track, the sky was burnt orange. There were three farm gates, and again he cursed Koetie for not being there to open them. Then, ahead, he recognised Majola's boy trotting along the track and he slowed down.

'Klim,' he said to him, indicating with his head for the boy to jump on the tailgate. The little bastard could do the gates.

When he was through the last gate, he didn't wait but left the boy to close it. It was then, as he looked across his lands in the early evening light, that he saw the donkeys grazing with his sheep and cattle in front of Majola's shack. Instantly the bees, which had swarmed in his head before he left town and which had settled with Steve Hofmeyr's voice, rose again, angrier than before.

Donkeys. On his land. When the veld was so dry. He would shoot them.

He skidded to a stop under the mesquite tree in front of the farmhouse, flung open the bakkie door, and then slammed it.

'Majolaaaaaa!' Baas Jan's voice echoed through the valley so that even the old hadeda that roosted in the mesquite cried out.

From faraway came the response: 'Myyyyyy baaaaaas!'

Jan unlocked the house, and dumped the meat and brandy on the kitchen table. A small black fruit bat lay dead in the middle of the floor and he kicked it outside. There were cobwebs, and he yanked the duvet off the bed to make sure there were no snakes under the covers.

Majola appeared from the bush when it was dark and Baas Jan had lit his braai fire and poured his brandy and Coke. He knew how to time these things.

'Naand, my basie,' said Majola from beyond the ring of light.

'Where the hell have you been?' said Baas Jan.

'My basie, I was in the veld, checking on my basie's sheep,' he lied.

'Whose donkeys are those?'

'It's my family, my basie – they came to visit but they are not staying very long, my basie,' he lied again.

'You tell them to take their filthy donkeys and go tonight because, if they are here tomorrow, I will shoot them.'

Majola said nothing.

'Hoor jy?'

'Ek hoor, Meneer,' Majola said.

'Gaan, five am we work.'

'Ja, Meneer.' Majola glanced at the wors and brandy. 'Did my basie bring 'n ietsie for me to eat?'

'In the bakkie, take it and bugger off.'

Majola found the flour and yeast, and slipped a couple of Baas Jan's cigarettes from the box on the passenger seat into his pants pocket. He saw the shotgun but avoided touching it. It would be a late start tomorrow, he thought. This man never rose before mid-morning when he came to the farm without his wife. He glanced back at Baas Jan who was staring into the flames, his brandy in one hand and the braai tongs in the other. Majola knew it wouldn't be long now and the shooting would start.

The blast of a shotgun woke them in the deepest part of the night. Majola stiffened as he listened to the ringing silence, and imagined Baas Jan reloading. Everyone and everything was awake now, eyes wide, ears cocked, ready to run. He knew Baas Jan wanted to show them all he was the boss on this farm and that he could make their lives hell. The mevrou would be on her stoep, Majola thought, peering into the dark.

At last, he dozed again, but the angry crashing of a man's boots approaching made him sit up. He knew the brandy was finished and Baas Jan was coming to soek for trouble in their hok.

In the moonlight Majola saw Baas Jan stumble closer. The karretjiemense had been asleep underneath the cart which he had helped them push up against the hok. They were awake too and he could see them moving out to hide in the bush.

'I told you to voetsak,' Baas Jan shouted. 'I am the baas here. I am going to shoot your filthy donkeys.'

Majola stepped towards him, his hands raised as if to make peace. He was bare-chested and bleary-eyed, but he had on his ragged blue overall pants.

'It's okay, my basie, these are respectful people – they will do what you want,' Majola said, his voice steady.

'Take your things and go. All of you!' Baas Jan was raging.

Majola saw the karretjiemense were still huddled behind the cart. The woman said softly to the child, 'Gaan, gaan,' pushing her into the darkness and she answered, 'Mamma, I am afraid.'

'Ja, ja, gaan, gaan. Voetsak! Blerrie kokkerotte,' Baas Jan shouted.

'It's very late, my basie,' Majola said quietly.

Baas Jan stared at him, perhaps trying to remember why he had come. He swayed but then leant on the shotgun as if it was a walking stick.

'I am going to shoot those fokken donkeys.' His speech was slurred, but he lifted the gun and pointed it at the silent shapes behind the cart. 'And then I am going to shoot you.'

'Nee, my basie, my brother is a very hard-working man – he will help us with the watermelons tomorrow. Go and rest now, we have a long day ahead.'

'And you, Majola, you think you are the boss of this farm, you think you call the shots here, but you and your whore are kokkerotte that nobody wants.'

He leered at Majola, as if he was trying to make out his face in the moonlight. When the spade came down on Baas Jan's head, it was with surprising force, as Majola knew Ou Ana hadn't eaten much for two weeks. With that single blow, she killed Baas Jan, and they all watched as his legs folded and he fell forwards and sprawled into the sand. The smell of brandy was all around them and then the karretjieman sniffed the air for something else. Majola knew he too had picked up the smell of urine. The moon had set; it was too dark for them to see Baas Jan's red-blue eyes or the blood trickling from his mouth.

Without a word, the two families came together over the body.

Majola prodded it with a toe.

'Hy's dood,' he said.

'What are we going to do now?' the karretjieman asked him.

'Bury him. Kom. Boetie, help here.'

The men turned Baas Jan on his back. Each man took an arm and they dragged the body away from the hok and into the brush. Ou Ana followed with the spade and Boetie carried Baas Jan's gun. The little karretjie girl and her mother came behind them. When Majola was satisfied that they were deep enough in the bush, they took turns digging a shallow grave and, with their feet, they rolled the body into the hole, which they covered with branches and rocks.

Without a word, they made their way to Baas Jan's house where the door stood open and the embers of his braai fire glowed. Ou Ana broke the leftover wors into six small pieces and they shared out the bread before they helped themselves to coffee, sugar, powdered milk, flour, yeast, and oil from the kitchen. Majola pocketed the rest of the cigarettes.

By the time the sun rose over the Swartberg, Majola, Ou Ana, and Boetie were asleep again, under their single blanket in the hok. In the field in front of them, the donkeys grazed undisturbed between the cattle and the sheep while mossies fought noisily over the crumbs they had dropped. Siena lay under the cart, her body pressed against her mother's warm back. She listened to the chattering mossies and the far-away crowing of a cock. For a little while she thought about the man the aunt had hit over the head with the spade; he had made her very afraid. But then, the pink-yellow apricot sweet in her mouth made her forget him, and she closed her eyes as her tongue touched its rough sugary edges. The rest of the sweets were buried in a hole she had dug with her fingers under the cart, right where she was now resting her head.

Chapter 4

Boetie narrowed his eyes, glaring at Siena.

'How old are you?' she asked.

He didn't answer.

'Boetie? Hey?'

He sighed loudly, like an old man being pestered by a nagging wife, stopped walking, and stared at the ground.

'It's not a hard question, you know,' she said.

'Sixteen,' he said, glancing at her and pursing his lips.

'Don't lie. If you are sixteen, you can make sex, and you don't know how to do that.'

'If I say I am sixteen, then I am sixteen,' he said, irritable. 'And I do know how to make sex.'

'Well, I am eight,' she said. 'The mevrou says I am eight.'

Numbers sounded like English, Boetie thought, words with meanings he didn't understand. He didn't know how old he was, but it had never been an issue. Until now – until Siena had made him tired with her questions and jabber, jabber, jabber. *Boetie, why? Boetie, what?* She quacked in a person's ears like the mevrou's fat ducks.

In truth, he knew he was too big for grade one, but Leroy was in grade three and said he was eleven. Maybe he was the same as Leroy; maybe he was eleven.

'I think you are eight, like me,' Siena said.

'I am not like you,' he said with a sneer. 'I don't stink like a donkey.' When she didn't respond, he said, 'Ja! Something that makes you quiet, hey, karretjiemeid.'

Boetie looked back at her but said nothing. His meanness surprised him but he didn't feel bad even though, since that time when the police took Ou Ana and Majola, Siena had played with him. The afternoon when they were arrested, he had been on the koppie and had watched the dust of approaching vehicles. It was a dust cloud he had known was inevitable and, instead of running to warn them, he'd stayed on his rock and watched. The police vans had stopped at the last farm gate and a blue figure had jumped out to open it. Then slowly, the line of white vans had bumped across the servitude. Majola, tall and upright, and then Ou Ana, small and bent, had come out of the hok, where they had been sleeping, and stood like dumb sheep, watching as the vans came closer. The policemen had poured from the vans like ants, crawling around the yard and into the hok. They'd patted down Ou Ana and Majola and pointed for them to climb into the back of a van. Its door had been locked behind them and, as suddenly as they had come, the vehicles had turned and bounced back along the servitude. The opening and closing of the gate had been repeated and then the dust cloud had reappeared. Just like that, the waiting was over and they were gone.

Boetie had gone back to the hok and taken Majola's knife from its hiding place on the small ledge above the door. He'd walked a few paces towards the servitude, but then stopped and went back for Ou Ana's fire-blackened coffee pot and tin mug, which he'd tied up in their blanket and slung over his shoulder. The sun was setting when he'd crossed the mevrou's land, but he'd walked on until he came to the road, and then walked through the night to where Majola had said the karretjiemense were camped. That night, all the way along that long road out of the valley, tears had streamed over his cheeks. When he'd picked up the donkeys' spoor at first light, a ring, as impenetrable as one made of long white pendoring,

3 4

had encircled his heart and his mind was focused only on survival.

Always the donkeys, Siena thought, always the comments about smelling like them. In her mind she saw them, Pienkie and Haas, and her fingers moved as if she were touching their soft grey muzzles and pulling on their giant ears. Since she could remember, they had been there. When she was a baby and couldn't sleep, Pa would lift her onto old Pienkie's back and she would lie with her cheek against her coarse warm hair, her fingers knotted in Pienkie's mane and sucking her thumb as the donkey wandered from bush to bush pulling at the hard leaves. No, truly, there was nothing wrong with smelling like a donkey.

Although he could be nasty, Siena liked Boetie's face. When he was distracted or concentrating on something, she secretly studied his eyes, which were round and brown and, she thought, always looked naughty. His mouth was big and his lips full, and when he smiled he made a person feel so happy. He loved to trick Pa and make him jump. Once, he'd laid a length of old black pipe as if it were a snake near a sheep trough, and, as Pa had bent to splash his face in the morning, Boetie'd shouted, 'P'sopie slang!' Pa had jumped with both feet in the air so that even Ma had laughed. Pa had picked up the pipe and chased Boetie, shouting that he was going to give him a 'blerrie harde pak', but Boetie was fast and Pa was sore and full of coughing, and couldn't catch him.

Boetie didn't go to school, but Siena thought he was very clever because he knew so many things. She liked playing with him, but sometimes he made her afraid. Sometimes he was like a cobra when it was disturbed, rearing up and watching with mean beady black eyes, and then coming in for the strike. Yes, Boetie could be like that.

'So, when is your birthday?' she said now as they trotted along the footpath to the waterfall. She wanted to improve his mood.

'Leave me alone with your girl questions. I don't have a birthday and I don't have a number of how many years I am, okay. Are you happy? Go and tell your boyfriend, Leroy, so you can laugh about me.' The track narrowed and, as they made their way deeper into the kloof, she was forced to walk behind him.

'Boetie, I won't do that. I am asking you because I want to give you a present.'

'What present?' He stopped again and turned around, his eyes alive.

'When we get back, I will give it to you.'

'Sjoe, a present!' He was happy again, and he ran, laughing and jumping from one side to the other of the leiwater furrow, which ran alongside the track, leading the mountain water to the farms below.

Siena knew her present would impress him. It was a tortoise shell she had found upside down in an aardvark burrow. Pa had said the tortoise must have fallen into the hole and landed on its back. Whatever happened was a long time ago because there was no sign of the tortoise any more – just its shell, which was rough and clogged with sand. Inside had been a perfect white egg that turned to powder when she touched it. She had cried, but Pa had said it was too old to be touched and would have vanished as soon as the shell was moved. When Siena had found that tortoise shell, she knew straight away she would give it to Boetie.

There were three pools at the top of the furrow; the first two were small and shallow, but the third was deep and dark. The waterfall cascaded off the rock face so that the dark pool swirled and foamed dangerously. Boetie went straight to the black and bottomless water and waded in, kicking at crabs as they scuttled under the rocks in the shallows. He grabbed one between a thumb and a finger, its pincers clawing the air, and Siena screamed and laughed.

'You must pasop, Boetie. Pa says there is a mermaid in that pool. If you swim too deep, she will grab your legs and pull you under.'

He smiled. 'I am going to grab the mermaid first and pull her out by her fish tail.' Siena knew he was trying to torment her, as he tossed the crab into the deep part of the pool and dived after it, swimming under the waterfall. 'Look, Siena, I am waiting for the mermaid. Are you scared? Hey? Why don't you come in? Can't you swim?'

Her heart was pounding, but she ignored him and settled in the shallow water to play in the mud, scooping it into a heap and dividing it into pies.

'Come eat, I am making roosterkoek,' she shouted. He dived again and swam back to the bank, and she offered him a mud pie, which he took and squeezed between his fingers.

'You know Majola told me Outa Dolos lives in the bush here,' he said.

'Who's that?'

'A very old man whose eyes burn red like coals when the sun goes down. If he catches a child here alone, he will eat them,' Boetie whispered, his eyes filling with menace. When he saw she was afraid, he laughed. 'So, when the mermaid pulls me under, you will have to run, because Outa Dolos will come with his red flaming eyes and bite your head off.'

'That's not true. There is no one called Outa Dolos – my pa would know him. But don't go deep, Boetie. The mermaid has grabbed many children by the ankles.'

Boetie's teeth were chattering, but he dived down and surfaced with another crab and then waded out to settle in the sun, trapping the clawing creature in a ring of small rocks and poking it with a stick.

'We must tell the mevrou you are living with us now and then you can come to school with me,' said Siena. She had been thinking about asking Pa if she could go to school, and she didn't want Boetie to be left out.

He sat up, dropped the crab onto the ground between his legs and, with lightning speed, cracked its shell with a rock. Hooking his finger into its broken body, he scooped out the flesh and ate it.

'Sies, Boetie, how do those things taste?' she said, pulling a face.

He smiled and chewed. 'Like your roosterkoek.' He pulled off a leg and snapped it between his teeth.

'If you come to school with me we can ride on the bus together and the mevrou will buy us each a new shirt and black school shoes.'

'I don't want to go to school.' He threw the smashed body of the crab into the pool and waded in again, looking for another.

'They give children food at school,' Siena said, 'shop bread and sweet coffee.'

'You go to school – then I can have peace and quiet here.'

Since they had come back into the valley, Pa had told no one Boetie was with them. Siena wondered what the mevrou was thinking when she stood on the farmhouse's stoep watching them play. Sometimes Boetie would stop what he was doing and look towards the farmhouse, and Siena knew he was checking to see if the mevrou was there.

Boetie was everywhere but nowhere. At night, he came in only after Pa blew out the candle. In the morning, Ma gave him roosterkoek and, when the mevrou gave them offal after a sheep was slaughtered, Ma let Boetie cook the liver for himself. Siena and Boetie took fruit from the orchard and

Boetie taught her to find muisvoël nests that were filled with small eggs, which he cracked open onto his waiting tongue.

Still, school was the dream that Siena wanted fulfilled with all her heart. Every day she wondered if that would be the day the mevrou would come and say it was time she joined the other children on the bus. She wanted to sit in the front, next to the driver, and say things to other girls like, 'Lend me a book,' or, 'Let me write it for you.' Learned people said things like that to one another.

Boetie came out of the pool and moved onto a rock in the sun to plait grass stalks. Siena moved closer to watch him. 'Make me one too,' she said when she saw he had made a small raft that he floated on the pool. He twisted more grass into shape and soon they were both in the shallows again, flicking their rafts across the water.

'Let's race them,' Boetie said, running to the furrow. 'Come, bring yours.'

They chased the spinning rafts along the fast, gurgling stream, sometimes jumping into the water to free them when they snagged on rocks or debris. When the rafts disappeared down a pipe, they ran ahead and waited impatiently for them to emerge. The game was fun and Siena squealed and laughed. Boetie too, for that little while, was unguarded and happy.

And then, as the furrow gurgled towards the farmhouse, they found an old tortoise. He was a giant, who, Siena heard afterwards, could have been more than a hundred years old. Boetie saw him first, standing in the rushing water, his ancient head turned upwards with his mouth open and gasping for air. They stopped, forgetting the rafts which rushed on towards the dam at the bottom of the valley.

'Ai siestog, he can't get out of the furrow,' said Siena, jumping into the water to heave the old tortoise out.

'Los.' Boetie grabbed her arm with a force Siena had never

felt before. 'Los,' he said again. And then, before she realised what he was doing, he picked up a rock and brought it down on the tortoise's shell so that both the ancient creature and the girl cried out together.

The mevrou found them when the tortoise was dead. Boetie was digging out its inside with a stick and Siena was standing over him, watching with fascination.

'What have you done?' the mevrou screamed, and Siena looked up in surprise and then shame. 'Dear God, what have you children done?'

Siena knew, when she heard the mevrou's voice and when she saw her father's wild eyes as he emerged from the bush where he had been spanning a fence, that this would change things. The mevrou shoved Boetie in front of her so that he stumbled while Pa held on to Siena's arm so that she had to run to keep up with him or be dragged. The other workers, who had heard the mevrou's wail, were running to the house. Siena felt a warm wetness trickle between her legs. Fear and mortification overwhelmed her, and her knees buckled so that Pa had to hold her up, his blunt black nails digging into her arm. On the last stretch, across the lawn where the children played on Sunday afternoons, she heard only her own gasping for breath.

Chapter 5

Siena watched Hannatjie hold the pencil. It was pinched between her fingers and thumb, obeying her without hesitation as she copied work from the blackboard onto the paper the teacher had handed out. Letters appeared like magic from its tip, and she wondered how they could mean things like they did to the teacher and the other children. Hannatjie rubbed something out, dusted the page with the back of her hand, and carried on writing. Siena breathed out and closed her eyes. All around her was the scratch-scratch of pencils as words poured from heads, down arms, and through pencils onto paper, while hers stayed blank. Hannatjie looked up and, when she saw Siena wasn't writing, kicked her ankle. Siena opened her eyes and looked at the boy on her other side, who was swinging his legs as he wrote. When he saw her watching him, he hid his work with a hand.

A tear splattered onto the blank sheet in front of her, smudging its pale blue lines.

'Do your work,' Hannatjie whispered, frowning.

Siena rubbed her eyes with her palms, then picked up the pencil that was lying in a groove at the top of the desk she was sharing with her new friend. It was the first time in her life she had held a pencil, and she turned it and looked at the point, testing the sharpness with a fingertip. Again, she studied how Hannatjie was holding hers. Siena manoeuvred it between her fingers and thumb, but it slipped and made a mark on the page. She picked it up again, gripping it in her fist and, with clenched teeth, carved her first letter, an 'O', like the one on the board, in the middle of the page between the mark and the wet splotch.

When she looked up to copy another easy one, the teacher was clip-clopping towards her and Siena dropped the pencil, which fell to the floor and rolled away. The class stopped writing and heads turned. She was shaking and she felt a pee coming, but, remembering the new pink broekies Aunt Esme had given her to wear and using all her mental strength, she focused on holding in her bladder. Her chin dropped to her chest, she wrapped her arms around her sides and squeezed her eyes closed so that red shapes swam into her mind. Her tears were unstoppable now, even with closed eyes, as she waited for the klap.

Fingertips touched the back of her neck like a moth. The teacher's soapy smell made her nose tickle, but still blood pounded in her ears, blocking out the silence of the classroom. The fingers prised a hand from her side, and Siena could feel the teacher's soft skin as she took Siena's hand in hers and turned the palm upwards. A nail traced a light circle on her flat hand that made her want to pull her hand back – not from fear but from a lightning bolt of pleasure.

'Round and round the garden goes the teddy bear …' The class joined in, and Siena became aware of Hannatjie giggling. 'One step … two step … tickle Siena there …' Keeping her head down, Siena peeped at the juffrou, who was bending over her, still holding her hand. She lifted her face, looked into the teacher's hazel eyes, and smiled, showing all her teeth.

'That's my girl,' the juffrou said. 'So you are also ticklish, hey? Hey? I must remember that.' She prodded Siena's ribs and she squealed. 'Hannatjie, ag, lovey, please pick up her pencil.'

Hannatjie leant down and looked under the desk. The

pencil was under the chair in front of them, and she rolled it back with her toes and picked it up.

'Thanks, lovey.'

The juffrou positioned the pencil between Siena's fingers and thumb and, using her own hand as a guide, they wrote the date and then Siena's name on the torn, damp sheet.

'You see the letter that looks like a snake lying in the veld?'

Siena nodded.

'That's a sss for "Siena". That word is your name – you wrote it.'

The class watched, fascinated by the gradual relieving of pressure. One by one they turned back to their papers and copied the words on the board. More pencils dropped and were returned by searching toes as chairs scraped.

'Sssss?' Siena said. She had never thought of it like that – that Siena and snake sounded the same.

'That's right. Now listen to me, Siena … No matter what anyone here tells you, nobody knew how to hold a pencil when they started school. It's my job to teach you. That's what school is. You are in grade one now. You are going to learn to read and write, but you have to keep your eyes open and listen. You can't give up and you can't cry, you hear?'

School. Grade one. Read. Write. She wanted to close her eyes and listen to the words roll across her mind like clouds in the sky, but the juffrou said she had to keep them open, so she nodded and smiled with her teeth again, and the juffrou patted her hand.

'Good girl.'

Siena studied her name on the paper.

'Sss,' she whispered. 'Sssnake, Sssiena … sssit, Sssiena … sssstand, Sssiena … sssalt, Sssiena … sssun, Sssiena … sssugar … Ssseekoegat … ssschool.'

There were many words she could learn to write if she

43

could make a snake-letter. This was easy. The juffrou was back at the board, making a long wavy line with her white chalk.

'Class, fill every line on your page with this river pattern. I want to see you touch the top and the bottom lines, but don't go over.'

She walked back to Siena and, again, showed her how to hold her pencil. This time, Siena got it right. She felt important now, like the cashier in Pep, who kept a pencil tucked behind an ear so she didn't lose it. Ma and Pa couldn't do this – they didn't even have a pencil – and now she could hold one like a geleerde mens and she had written her name. She filled the page with rivers, sometimes going out the lines, then turned it over and made snakes, so that by the end of the lesson she could make an 'S' without looking at the board.

'You are lucky,' Hannatjie said at break time. 'You have a short name with easy letters but I have a mouthful. Why didn't my ma call me Sana or Lisa, or something like that, but Hannatjie. Joh! What kind of a name is that?'

'Why is your name Hannatjie?'

'I don't know. They just call me that. It's not my birth certificate name. That's Henrietta-Lyn, but I don't like that either.'

'Henrietta-Lyn is a very fancy name. You should tell everyone that's your name.'

'Oh no, then I am going to have to learn to write it and I have only just got Hannatjie right.'

'My name is really Elisabeth. I am very glad juffrou doesn't know that – I think it would be a difficult one to write.'

'Yes, but not as hard as Hannatjie. Hannatjie is a very long name. It must be a record for this school!'

They laughed for a long time, and then Siena fetched the fresh paper and pencil stub the juffrou had let her take from class and which she had hidden under her pillow in the dormitory. For the rest of the afternoon, she crouched on

44

beginning of the world. If you eat a tortoise, everything we know will be forgotten. Never mess with a tortoise.'

Now, at school, Siena thought about Pa and what he had said. She thought of Boetie and the old tortoise they had killed, with its gasping toothless mouth and broken eyes. What had they done? She had seen a tortoise's only tear, and afterwards everything changed. It was true what Pa said – a tortoise was the spirit of the veld; she should have listened to him.

Siena sat every afternoon on the steps outside the classroom, watching the veld and waiting for the sun to drop away, as rivers rolled down her cheeks plopping into the dry sand between her feet. She and Boetie had killed that tortoise, and she knew for sure they had changed the way of things forever.

'Forgive me, wise tortoise, my pa's friend. It was me, Siena, who made you cry your only tear. It should have been me who protected you. It should have been me. I am sorry.'

The children at Seekoegat Primary stayed away from her when she cried, but always Aunt Esme sent Hannatjie to sit with her.

'Just put an arm around her shoulders, Hannatjie. That's what friends must do,' Aunt Esme said. Hannatjie would sit in silence listening to Siena weep and then, in her teacher-voice, she would make her laugh.

'One step … two step … tickle Siena there!'

It seemed then the old tortoise could be forgotten, but he always came back, in the dark hours when she was the only one awake. Siena would lie in bed with her hands under her head and watch the stars through the window. It felt like forever before Aunt Esme began clearing the coals out the stove and she smelt the wood smoke. It was then she knew night was finished and the kettle was on.

At school, Siena's life was run by routine. On waking, all the children went to the kitchen and had coffee. On warm days, they sat along the stoep at the kitchen door, sipping from their plastic cups. Afterwards, Aunt Esme filled a bucket of soapy water and each one rinsed their mug and put it back on the kitchen table, upside down, to dry. It was washing-the-body-time next. The boys and girls went to their dormitories and soaped their wet cloths to wash from top to toe before rinsing under the cold shower. When they were dressed, in their white shirts and grey pants, they folded their blankets at the foot of their bed and lined up for pap and a spoon of sugar. They rinsed their bowls in the bucket and then, when everything was cleared away, they lined up again and Aunt Esme squeezed toothpaste on each one's toothbrush, and they brushed their teeth and rinsed their mouths at the outside tap. Siena was given a red toothbrush and told to remember her colour. Aunt Esme collected the brushes when they were done. Despite having strong white teeth, Siena had never brushed before, but Hannatjie showed her how. At first, the Colgate burnt her mouth and she spat it out, but Aunt Esme was watching her and made her do it again.

'In this school, all children wash with soap and brush their teeth. My rules are my rules.'

Before lessons, they stood in front of Meneer Maans and bowed their heads as he prayed and read from the Bible. They finished with a song about Jesus, and then they split into the two classes. The juffrou took the beginners, and Meneer Maans the older boys, who were also beginners but who gave the juffrou a hard time. There were fourteen children, including Siena, and, although the school went up to grade six, very few made it that far. Every day, a different child was given the job of ringing the bell and they stopped their lessons for break. Two hours later, the bell was rung again for lunch, which was always cabbage or beans with rice. On a Sunday, they had chicken and potatoes. The boere sometimes brought offal or stewing mutton, and that was all the meat they ate. At night, it was roosterkoek, which Aunt Esme braaied over a fire at the kitchen door. Siena always left the bread. The food overwhelmed her and she felt she had eaten more at school than she had in her whole life. Her stomach cramped constantly; she was amazed how the other children were always hungry. She loved the coffee the most.

'This school always has coffee and milk and sugar,' she said to Hannatjie. 'Meneer Maans and Aunt Esme must be very rich to go to the shops for those things all the time.'

'It's the government's coffee,' Hannatjie said. 'The boere give the government the money to buy it for us.'

'Joh! Boere give away their money? Are you sure?'

'Yes, they have to. If the government says it wants some of their money, then they have to give it. But they don't mind because the boere have all the money in the whole world.'

Siena thought about what Hannatjie had said. 'I think you are right. For sure it is the only way this school always has a twenty rand to give us coffee with milk and sugar every day.'

'I know I am right – Aunt Esme told me that.'

After their lessons, the boys played soccer on a sand pitch behind the school, and the girls played netball or sat under the pepper tree behind their dorm and braided one another's hair. On Saturday mornings, Aunt Esme filled the washing-up bucket with warm water and placed a slab of green soap next to it at the kitchen door. She stood over them, hands on hips, as each child washed their school shirt and underpants, then hung them on the fence near the road.

Meneer Maans and the juffrou were not at school at weekends. They would drive off on the tar road to Oudtshoorn to visit their families and buy groceries for the next week. At these times, when they were alone, Aunt Esme taught them hopscotch and skipping games, and read to them from the Bible.

Even the big boys, the ones who gave the juffrou a hard time, listened to Aunt Esme.

'Why are you at this school?' Siena asked Hannatjie one weekday afternoon when they were under the pepper tree. The juffrou had bought Hannatjie a packet of hair extensions, and Hannatjie was trying to work them into Siena's very short hair. For a long time, Hannatjie didn't say anything but Siena, who understood silence, waited.

'My ma died,' she said eventually.

Siena kept her head down as Hannatjie wove in an extension. It was sore, but she didn't complain.

'My pa is on the farm, but I didn't like it there without my ma. Everyone hits me. They smoke dagga on the farm and my pa drinks papsak, and then the klaps come. When Ma was there, she never let him klap me.'

'Why does he hit you?'

'Pa says it is to make sure I am not naughty, but I think it makes him feel strong to klap a person who screams and cries. And then when he started with me, they all started, and sometimes they wouldn't stop.'

'Hannatjie, it's good you are here with us. Aunt Esme and Meneer Maans won't let anyone klap you.'

'It's funny, hey – when you are small they tell you that if you are naughty they will send you to school so the teacher can give you a hiding, but now we are at school, and the people here are the ones who have to help us to forget the hidings we got at home.'

For a while, neither of them spoke. And then, again, the old tortoise came into Siena's mind.

'I did something very bad and the mevrou said I had to come here.'

'What?'

'I had a friend called Boetie and we killed a tortoise.'

'You are here because you killed a tortoise? Is that all?'

'It's a very bad thing, Hannatjie.'

'Ag nee, on the farm we killed tortoises all the time and no one was sent away. That's stupid. Will you go home in the holidays?'

'Can a person go back?'

Hannatjie burst out laughing. 'Siena, this isn't jail. It's just school. We all go home in the holidays.'

Siena stared at her. 'Really?'

'Ja, did you think you would never go home again?'

Ma? Pa? She thought the mevrou had sent her away forever.

'When, Hannatjie? When is it the holidays?'

'Still a few weeks. But don't worry, Aunt Esme will help us get ready.' Hannatjie patted her head. 'Now sit still and let's see if I can give you braids. You can't look like a karretjiemeid for the rest of your life.'

It was then that a car turned off the tar road and they both looked up.

'Who's that now?' Hannatjie said.

It pulled up, and a man and a boy climbed out. The boy was barefoot and, from their place under the pepper tree, the girls could see he was dirty and his eyes were swollen so that they were small slits. The boy stood outside the car, not sure of where to go but the man ignored him.

'He looks like a mafella,' Hannatjie said. 'Meneer Maans won't like that.'

The man had a file full of papers, and he made his way to the path between the classrooms and the dormitories. The boy looked around and, when he saw the girls, he stopped and stared at them.

'Kriekie, come on,' the man shouted, but the boy took no notice. The man marched back, taking the boy's arm and pulling him along. The boy didn't resist, but did not take his eyes off the girls.

'Meneer Maans doesn't take mafella in this school,' said Hannatjie. 'This is a school for special cases, not rubbish. That boy is not a case for Seekoegat Primary.'

'I wonder,' said Siena, who was thinking about grade one, 'if that boy has ever held a pencil?'

'Siena, he is a street child, a mafella. He has never seen soap and water, never mind a pencil.'

'No, he is not a mafella,' said Siena. 'Something has happened to him, just like something happened to us.'

Chapter 6

Kriekie crawled into the aardvark burrow, which, despite the rocky veld, was cushioned by soft sand. If he looked over its mouth, he could see the lights of traffic on the N1 freeway and hear the squealing of brakes as heavily loaded trucks slowed down when they approached the truck stop. Dolly, his mother, once told him the trucks were going to Cape Town and they travelled over high mountains to get there. When he'd asked her where they had come from, she'd said, 'Joburg.' The truckers had told her that themselves but Joburg, like Cape Town, was a place Dolly had never seen.

He slept in the burrow when Dolly took the once-a-day train to anderkant Beaufort West. She never asked Kriekie where he slept or what he ate when she was gone. Maybe she thought he stayed under the afdak they rented from an aunt in one of the houses near the station. Still, he knew she was always happy to see him waiting for her when she climbed off the train.

Tonight was cold, and for a while he had sat under the af-dak outside the aunt's house wrapped in their blanket. When the moon rose, he pushed the blanket into the corner with their other things and walked into the veld. A barbed-wire fence spanned all the way along the back of the houses, but it hung loose where people climbed through and, despite the problem with his hands, he slipped through easily. Behind the houses, the veld was littered with plastic and glass and the rusted shell of a car from long ago that lay on its roof. Soon, he was away from the settlement and the smell of burning rubbish and diesel fumes that hung over it.

Kriekie loved the veld in the grey light. He imagined he was an animal and, when he felt like running, he became a Karoo hare or, if he felt tired, he would be a tortoise. When he was hungry, he was always a porcupine. Regtig, he thought, porcupines were always looking for food. Tonight, he had been an aardvark making its way back home. The burrow was one of the deepest he had found, and he was able to wriggle down the tunnel so that his body was completely hidden. He had found it while walking in the veld on one of the days when Dolly was gone, and had cleared out the loose rocks and then marked it in a way that he could find it again. He never thought a snake or a scorpion might be inside and he was lucky. It was abandoned and unoccupied. It was his special place and, when he was inside, he curled up and slept, not so much like an aardvark but more like a feral kitten.

Sometimes, when he had that feeling of wanting Dolly, he sang. Dolly sang all the time, but he didn't know any real songs so he made them up and they were always about Dolly going on the train and himself, whom people from the settlement called Kriekie, staying behind. For the two days and three nights she was gone every week, he didn't go back to the afdak. There was a sheep's trough in the veld not far from the burrow where he drank, and during the day he looked for things to eat. There wasn't anything in the veld, but sometimes the aunts in the houses gave him bread, or the drivers at the truck stop let him lick the last of their pap and sauce out their bakkies. Once, when a group of men, speaking a language he had never heard, were braaiing, one of them gave him wors.

Kriekie knew there were jackal and rooikat in the veld but they never bothered him. He could hear the jackal crying in the night, and he wondered if it was because they were also hungry. The rooikat avoided him, but he knew if sheep were nearby, the rooikat were there too, and that sooner or later he would hear the rumble of the farmer's bakkie and with it the crack-crack of a shotgun. He never worried about any of them. It was the boys from the brick houses at the siding who made him afraid.

He'd been afraid since that day, when Dolly was gone, when he had run alongside the Shosholoza Meyl shouting up at the passengers who were thinking Joburg and Cape Town stories when he needed them to be seeing that this Karoo boy needed something to eat. 'Sweets, some sweets …' He'd clapped his hands and pointed at his mouth so they would get the message. When the train squealed and shuddered and stopped, he saw a little girl at an open window.

'Hullo, seuntjie,' she'd called down.

'Meisie … Sweets, sweets, sweets,' he'd shouted.

There had been other boys begging from the train, some of them helping one another to leap at the open windows where they hung on with one hand to grab what they could with the other, but these boys were further down the line. Kriekie always begged from the carriage behind the locomotive because, when the train came through, it was the middle carriages that stopped in the station directly in front of the houses. The locomotive was far ahead on the line that stretched into the veld so nobody, except him, bothered with the first carriage.

'I am Sunette,' she said. 'Do you want food, seuntjie?'

'Throw for me sweets, throw for me sweets!'

She disappeared into the compartment and, as the whistle blew, she came back and tossed out an open packet of Jelly Tots, then watched as he scrambled to pick up the pink and green and yellow sweets in the dust. He never saw the two boys who were on top of him before he could run for it. There was no talking, just snatching. They grabbed the packet, and then worked to prise open his fingers to get the few he had picked up off the ground. He kept his fists tight until one of the boys came at him with a rock. His fingers, first on one hand and then the other, opened as the boy brought the rock down on his knuckles and the other boy held him down. They snatched the jelly tots as they rolled into the dust again, stuffing them into their mouths. The train shuddered and squealed again and, from where he lay, Kriekie looked up at Sunette's carriage window. She was still there, her blue eyes fixed on him, but then, as the train picked up speed, someone reached over her and closed the window. He lay next to the track and watched the train disappear around the bend.

It was where Dolly had found him and, when she saw his broken fingers, she swore and lifted him onto his feet. They'd walked back to the afdak together, him holding his bloodied hands curled in towards his chest and Dolly with a hand on his shoulder. She'd asked the aunt in the house for water and, for the rest of the day, he had sat with his hands in the bucket, thinking only about the pain and if it would ever end.

He was thinking about that now when there was snuffling close by the burrow and he looked up into the grey whiskery face of a porcupine. He reached up with his crooked fingers to touch its twitching nose, but it hissed and raised its quills, and, by the time he uncurled and peeped over the top of the burrow, it had disappeared. Once, on a night like this, he had seen wild horses. The breeze had been away from them, and he had watched their grey shapes, stamping and snorting, pick at the bushes. In the morning, they were gone, but he'd found their spoor and their droppings, and thought they must belong to the farmer. The horses were something Dolly would like, he thought, not to touch them but to see. She wouldn't believe there were horses so close by and he knew she would say, 'Joh, maar hulle's mooi!' and that would make him burst with joy.

Dolly always came back on the Monday train, unless she caught a lift on a truck. After that day with his hands, Kriekie didn't run for sweets any more, but he still waited for the train on the Cape Town-bound side of the tracks. He waited for Dolly, and he watched for Sunette, but he never saw her again. The day Dolly came back was his favourite day because she brought bread and red cooldrink and sometimes chips. If she made good money they had offal too, and he loved those days when Dolly made a fire and they had their own pot cooking. He knew the smell of the offal cooking made the people in the houses hungry and that this time it was for him and Dolly. They would eat together from the pot, talking and laughing, and she would tell him about Beaufort West and its houses and cars and big shops.

In the days after the offal, Dolly would drink and, when she came back from the shebeen, she would curl up under their blanket and sleep like she was dead. Kriekie didn't mind. He worked his way into her arms so that his back was against her breasts and they would stay there until she rose again to get more wine. When the money was finished, her eyes would change. All she wanted was to get to Beaufort West again. If he got too close or asked if he could come with her, she would chase him and hit him. Eventually, she would slip into a carriage on the Shosholoza Meyl, which passed on its way back to Joburg in the evening, and he would be alone again.

On the days when she was gone, Kriekie asked the lady in the shop at the truck stop if it was Monday yet.

'Two slapies,' she would say, or, 'Just one more slapie. Today is church day and tomorrow is school day. That's Monday.' Kriekie didn't know church or school; he'd been to neither. The church was in Leeu-Gamka, between him and

Dolly in Beaufort West, so when he saw the boere coming off the farms in their black Sunday cars, the men in suits and the women in pale blue and pink, and turning for Leeu-Gamka, he secretly sent Dolly messages with them.

'Come back early …'

'Bring green cooldrink this time …'

'Fetch me …'

The messages could travel on top of the cars, he thought, his secret messages that nobody knew were there.

This morning, it had been three slapies and, like yesterday, he had been at the station before sunrise in case the Shosholoza Meyl came early, as it sometimes did. As usual, the white car from town was parked, waiting for the post.

Dolly wasn't on the train again and, when the white car pulled out and disappeared back towards the mountains, he wandered into the veld, making his way to the rusted car wreck where he played for a while. Maybe she was coming on a truck. The next morning – four slapies – the train came and went and still there was no sign of her. It was just the white car waiting for the town's post; no one got on or off.

Kriekie knew something was wrong. He went to the truck stop shop and asked the lady if she knew where Dolly could be.

'Is she still not back?' He saw her frown and he hoped he hadn't made it so that Dolly would be in trouble. 'I am sure she is coming, don't worry. I will phone Beaufort West and ask them to tell her to get a move on. Take a blikkie milk and a half-loaf, okay – that will make you feel better.'

'Dankie, Aunt,' he said.

He sat in the doorway and drank the milk so the other boys wouldn't take it off him. When he was finished, he hid the half-loaf under his shirt and skirted the settlement, returning to the burrow. The milk had filled him, so he kept the bread for later. He was reluctant to leave the bread in case some animal sniffed it out and he would have nothing. All there was to do was sleep, so he crawled back inside and, as the sun climbed higher in the cloudless blue, he slept. The only sign he was there was a footprint in the soft sand at the burrow mouth.

The next morning, when he was back for the train again, the truck stop lady was watching for him and she beckoned for him to come to her.

'Luister, Kriekie, Dolly is not coming back today,' she said.

'Did she forget about me?' he asked.

'Of course not! She said to tell you she never stops thinking about you, but she has been held up in Beaufort West with her work. She asked me to arrange with the welfare to find a safe place for you to live so the welfare man is coming later. Have you got things you need to take with you?'

'Where is he taking me, Aunt?'

'He has very kindly found a bed for you at the school in Seekoegat. Dolly will be very pleased, because she says you are so clever and you should be in school. Also, it's on the Beaufort West road so she can find you easily when she is ready.'

He thought he should go back to the afdak and fetch their pot and blanket so that the aunt in the house didn't steal it. There was also the box with Dolly's clothes and identity book. She would be worried about that.

'Aunt, I must fetch Dolly's ID book. If she comes and I don't have it, she will klap me.'

'Okay, Kriekie, go fetch your stuff and come back here. I am going to make tea and put out some Marie biscuits for us while we wait for the welfare man. Don't be long now.'

Kriekie was excited. Tea and Marie biscuits were for town people. Maybe it was for the welfare man to eat while he waited outside. He didn't think the lady would really give him tea or let him eat her Maries. At the afdak, he pushed the pot into the box with Dolly's clothes and the ID book, and carried it back to the truck stop. Then he ran back to fetch their blanket.

'Put your things there at the door,' the lady said. 'Come along, you can have your tea at the back here with me. I have put in three sugars today and there are two Maries next to the cup for you.'

Kriekie's eyes went wide. He had never been behind the grill that separated the lady from her customers.

'Where are your clothes and your jersey?'

He couldn't find words so he shook his head. 'Bloody Dolly, always liked her wine more than looking after her children. My magtig! Okay, don't worry. The school will give you clothes.'

A chipped mug was steaming on a small table covered in a blue plastic sheet in the back corner. Radio Gamkaland was playing church music, and he sat down on a bankie covered in a sheep skin, feeling that today he was important. The lady, who sat opposite him, had a cup of tea too, but she had to keep standing up to serve customers who came to the grill wanting tobacco and chips. Because he couldn't pick up the cup with his curled hands, he leant over and slurped his tea, letting the Maries dissolve on his tongue one bite at a time. Boxes of chocolates were stacked well out of reach of the customers along the back wall, and below them were racks of chips. The cigarettes were packed neatly under the till. There was a Coke fridge and next to it two chest freezers. Kriekie wondered what was inside them, and who would ever have so much money that they could buy all these things.

He finished his tea and tried to lick out the undissolved sugar from the bottom of the mug. Seeing he was frustrated when he couldn't reach it, the lady, who had sat down again, handed him her teaspoon.

'Ai, Kriekie, you are a basket case,' she said and he smiled so sweetly, she gave him another Marie biscuit. 'Ai, and a little charmer too.'

A car pulled up outside and they both stood.

'Well, here's your ride,' she said.

The welfare man thanked the truck stop lady, gave her his cell number, and took Dolly's ID book.

'Phone me directly if there is news,' he said. She nodded and he winked.

He paid for two Cokes and two Lunch Bars, placing the packet on the floor behind his seat before opening the boot for Kriekie's box.

'Reg, ou maat, let's get you sorted!'

'You don't need the blanket,' he said when Kriekie ran to fetch it. 'Where you are going there are plenty of blankets.'

'It smells like Dolly,' Kriekie said.

The lady saw the panic on Kriekie's face and said: 'I will keep it and give it to Dolly when she comes. She will want to smell your smell too.'

When they pulled onto the N1, the welfare man said: 'Sleep if you want – it's a long road.'

The truck stop lady waved, but Kriekie didn't look back. He had noticed the switches and knobs on the dashboard, and was watching how the welfare man was turning and pushing things for cool air and then for music. For the first time in his life, Kriekie was in a car for his own trip.

Outside the truck stop shop, old Piet Hout, the worker who chopped the braai wood for the garage, stopped swinging his axe and watched them go. 'What happened to Dolly?' he asked Marina Visagie, who was still waving at the disappearing car.

'The police found her body in the veld anderkant Beaufort West. Raped and strangled.'

'Ag nee man,' old Piet Hout said. 'Who would do something like that now?'

'These prostitutes working the N1 don't live long,' the truck stop lady said. 'If AIDS doesn't get them, something else does. Anyway, it's a blessing for this child – she was a useless mother.'

She turned to go back inside and saw the old blanket lying in a heap at the door where Kriekie had left it. In its folds was a small square photograph of Dolly standing in front of a spekboom holding a baby.

'Do me a favour, Piet, burn this – it's crawling with lice.'

She went back into the shop, put the picture in the pages of her Bible, cleared the mugs, and packed away the Marie biscuits.

Chapter 7

Siena listened to the wind. *It's like an angry man*, she thought, *with a voice that grows louder and louder before smashing and smacking.* She closed her eyes, pulled the grey blanket over her head, and tried to doze. The door rattled, and dust and the dried-out flowers from the giant purple bougainvillea gusted in through the broken window, settling on the curled-up sleeping girls. Every few seconds a thorny branch from the tree in the backyard whacked the tin roof of the Seekoegat dormitory, and she wondered how the others slept so easily. The cold crept from her feet, along her legs and into her bones, and she blew into her hands and pulled her knees into her chest so her body was a ball. If she moved the blanket slightly down, she could see the sky through the broken window and still keep her ears and nose covered. There were no stars this morning, which meant the cloud had moved off the mountains. The Swartberg would be white today; it felt like a snow wind. Next to her, Hannatjie snored gently through her snotty nose, and Siena pushed one foot out of the warmth to kick her, which made the girl cough and roll over.

As the room turned grey, she heard the familiar scraping coming from the kitchen. Aunt Esme was up and cleaning the ash from the wood stove before she made the fire. Soon, steam would be pouring from the big yellow-and-green enamel kettle while Aunt Esme spooned in coffee, milk powder, and sugar. That was the lekker thing about school – sweet white coffee. Every day.

Her dream had woken her again, the same one that woke her every night. Boetie was laughing while he threw klippies at Baas Jan, who was alive and shooting in the air with his big gun. She was in the dream too, pulling Boetie's arm, begging him to come so they could catch up to Ma and Pa and the old tortoise who were riding away on the karretjie. Boetie kept escaping her grip, laughing and running off, all the while picking up klippies. It was always the crack-crack-crack of Baas Jan's big gun that woke her up.

Aunt Esme said the dream was nothing to worry about. She said Siena needed to sort out what to remember and what to forget and, until her mind had done that, she would keep having her dream. But every night, even when she thought things were sorted out, she woke up with the crack-crack-crack in her ears, her heart racing, calling out Boetie's name. Some nights the old tortoise's face appeared instead of Boetie's laughing black eyes, its ancient, milky eyes always filled with tears. When the dream first started, Hannatjie had climbed into bed with her and Siena held on to her so she wouldn't be afraid. After a few nights, the other girl became irritated by her restlessness and went back to her own bed. All Siena could do then was listen for Aunt Esme's clucking and crowing on the other side of the wall, and watch for the morning star through the broken window.

She wrapped the grey blanket around her shoulders and stood up. She had on the yellow nightie, which came down to her knees, with the pink dog on the front. Meneer Maans had bought all the girls one at Pep. Her feet were bare. The bolt on the metal door opened easily, but the wind banged it hard against the wall, and she quickly looked to see if the little ones had woken up. Her time with Aunt Esme was special; she didn't mind Hannatjie, but she wanted the others to stay asleep. Keeping close to the building, Siena ran to the kitchen where an oil lamp was burning and Aunt Esme was on one knee feeding wood into the roaring fire she had started in the old stove.

'Hullo, Aunt,' she said, 'can I have coffee?'

The old woman looked up when she heard Siena's voice. 'Ja, my ou Klimmie. Have you been dreaming of your boyfriend? Is that why you are up so early?'

'Ja, Aunt, he was with the crying tortoise again.'

'Aitog. You children should never have killed that tortoise. Its spook is going to haunt you for the rest of your life.'

Siena stood near the stove, her teeth chattering.

'It's holidays already, Aunt. I will see Ma and Pa again.'

Aunt Esme smiled. 'Ja, this year's going too fast. You are growing up, Klimmie. One of these days you will want to leave us. A clever girl like you can't stay in Seekoegat forever. Hey! You children creep into my heart and then I must let you go.'

'Ja, Aunt. I told the meneer I want to go to Swartberg school. I am going to try for high school.'

'That's my ou Klimmie. Maybe you will be a teacher one day.'

The old woman fetched two mugs from the cupboard and, using a dishcloth, lifted the boiling enamel coffee pot off the stove and filled the mugs with the sweet milky brew.

'P'sop, this is hot, nè,' she said, handing Siena the mug.

'Ja, Aunt.'

'You must wash early. That welfare man comes just when he likes. Now, what will you do when you get to town? Wait at the BP for the valley school bus as usual?'

Siena nodded. It was a long trip and the welfare man always had a car full of Klaarstroom boys going with him to town. Last time, the car became stuck in sand and they all had to get out and push. The trip on the school bus was worse.

Leroy always pinched her and, if she screamed, the oom pulled over and klapped her. Maybe today the oom would let her sit in front.

The lamp flickered as the door opened and the other children came in, all of them running to the wood stove, coughing and sniffing and rubbing their hands. Siena set out more mugs, which Aunt Esme half-filled with coffee. When every child had a mug, Aunt Esme settled them on Siena's grey blanket in front of the wood stove. The previous night, before they went to bed, she had set the big black pap pot next to the stove, ready to make breakfast. Now, Siena fetched a half-bucket of water from the sink and took the mielie meal out the cupboard. It was the last day of term, and there was plenty to do.

The day-school transport from town to the valley was a pale blue minibus the oom had bought from a taxi man in Oudtshoorn. Each morning during term, he collected the children who went to day school from the farms along the valley road, stopping every few kilometres to load another one or two. He returned them in the afternoon, a round trip for the oom of one hundred and forty kilometres. The bus broke down often. Its smooth tyres usually picked up a puncture on the stony road, or it ran out of petrol, or it overheated on the climb up the last hill before the oom freewheeled into the valley. If it stopped near the end of the road, the children who lived on the mevrou's farm, and who took up most of the seats on the bus, walked the rest of the way.

Siena hated the school transport; the oom was always bad tempered, and the farm boys fought the whole way. The smaller girls hid under the seats and, if one of the high-school girls came home from boarding school, she sat in front. There was nowhere an ordinary girl, who wasn't little or big, could sit in peace. Today, though, Siena was in luck. The oom chased

Leroy into the back seat so Siena could sit in front. The bus made it up the last hill, and the road had been scraped, so for once they didn't pick up a puncture. When they eventually arrived at the farm gate, there was still an hour of daylight. The melting snow meant the river was flowing. Siena took off her shoes, tucked her skirt into her panties, and waded into the ice-cold water, holding her bag and shoes above her head.

She loved holidays on the farm when she played the old games she had once played with Boetie. He had been good at finding Hottentot-figs, and she remembered how once they had climbed the baboon's ridge. Pa had said they would be able to see all the way to Fraserburg if they did it on a clear day. On top, they hadn't found Fraserburg but they had seen the faraway highway with its big trucks. In the years since the tortoise thing she had missed Boetie and his fancy plans. Now, though, there was Sussie, who would be sitting up and, Siena thought, maybe even showing signs of crawling.

Pa was waiting for her, sitting on a rock smoking, as she picked her way through the stream. When she saw him, she dropped her bag and shoes on the riverbank, and ran into his arms.

'You are fat,' he teased, pinching her cheeks.

'And you are skraal,' she laughed, squeezing his bony shoulders. 'How are Ma and Sussie?'

'Ma is very happy you are home – I think she is tired of jumping up and down for Sussie. That one is worse than a boy. Regtig!'

Siena smiled and Pa picked up her school bag. 'Put on your shoes and carry your bag. You are a proper school pupil now and Ma wants to see how you look. She will be very proud to have a child with a bag full of books.'

And I can read them now, she thought, all the anger and drama of her being sent away to school long forgotten.

'So is Sussie sitting now?'

'She is sitting and demanding!'

They laughed again, and Siena breathed in Pa's wood-smoke and tobacco smell.

'And Boetie, Pa? Did you find out any news?" She looked around, still laughing, half expecting Boetie to leap from behind a rock or a bush. 'Is he here? Did the mevrou say he could visit? I want to climb the baboon's ridge again, remember we spoke about it, Pa?'

Pa didn't answer and Siena felt his mood shift. She searched his face, wanting to understand why he was so quiet. Boetie had been her best friend – his naughty face, his schemes, their expeditions into the veld had been exciting.

'Boetie is gone from us forever, my Sienatjie. He is with his mother's people there by the station on the N1. It is better for a boy to stay with his own people and not run unsupervised, getting up to no good here in the valley. The mevrou never wanted him around here anyway after the thing with Baas Jan and then the tortoise.'

They walked on without talking, the happy moment of homecoming over. Boetie must hate living on the highway, Siena thought. Once, when they were on the karretjie, Pa had steered the donkeys onto the N1, and they had nearly been killed by a truck that bore down on them, hooter blaring. The donkeys had swerved into the veld and the karretjie had tipped over. It was the only time Pa had taken them on the tar road. There were no mountains or rivers, just the N1 and its trucks and cars. Boetie didn't make friends easily, Siena thought – except for her because she understood him. She knew what he was like.

'It's better this way,' Pa said. 'You are growing up and the mevrou said you are doing so well at Seekoegat Primary. You must play with Leroy and his sister. They haven't grown up seeing what Boetie has seen. Forget about Boetie. Anyway he will be getting big, my Sienatjie. He won't be the same boy you remember. Regtig, it is better this way.'

Siena smiled at Pa and took his arm. 'It's okay, Pa. I want to be with Ma and Sussie and you anyway. Boetie was a pain sometimes. He always wanted me to do his boy things. I like being at home and not climbing mountains. I was scared of the baboons anyway.' They both laughed.

'Ma has made roosterkoek, and I bought a blikkie jam and batteries for the radio. It will be a good holiday for you. Come on, now, I want you to be happy.'

'I am happy, Pa. I am happy to be with you all.'

Across the field, Siena could see Ma's shape bent over a fire and she could hear Sussie crying. Yes, Boetie was gone, and, deep inside, Siena felt herself letting go and with it came unexpected relief.

Chapter 8

There was no way to climb the wall of the prison. Boetie walked around the side, looking for a way over, but it was impenetrable. If only he were a lizard. He jumped at the rough surface, willing his hands and feet to stick. Tattered plastic bags hung like flags on the curls of barbed wire that stretched along the top. What he didn't know was that many others had paced this same wall before him, looking for footholds and, failing that, trying to throw parcels over or calling to someone inside. There was singing on the other side of the wall, and he could smell pap cooking. Again, he walked the periphery, looking all the time for something he could grab on to.

'Ou Ana!' he shouted. 'Ou Ana!' He stopped pacing and cocked an ear; still, there was only the singing. Then, much closer, pots were moved and the steamy smell of the pap became stronger so that his stomach growled.

'Ou Ana! Are you there?' His voice faded. No one was listening. It was no use.

Before he'd crossed the mountains and come to Oudtshoorn, he had knocked on the heavy jail door facing the main street in town and the warden who had opened it recognised him.

'What do you want?'

'I need to see Ou Ana.'

'She is not here. She is in Oudtshoorn for court.'

'Then where is Majola?'

'You know he is in Pollsmoor. If a person kills somebody then we send him to live with all the other murderers in Cape Town.'

'I want Ou Ana.'

'Ag, Jirre … then go to Oudtshoorn.' Boetie closed his eyes as the door slammed in his face. He leant against it, listening to the warden's chair scraping as he sat down again.

Go to Oudtshoorn, the warden had said. Boetie had never been beyond the outlying farms of the district. He knew Klaarstroom and Majola had once taken them to a farm near Rietbron. Leroy had been to Oudtshoorn for school athletics, and when he came home he had been a big deal because the mevrou had given him five rand for ice cream. Boetie remembered that because he had wanted more than anything to change places with Leroy then, to be in school and going to Oudtshoorn with the mevrou giving him ice-cream money.

Ou Ana must be glad to be in a big town, he thought. People only went to Oudtshoorn for very important things. Like school athletics or to go to hospital. Or court. He would go to Oudtshoorn, he decided, because finding Ou Ana was important, and when he found her then everything would be okay.

On that day, which seemed so long ago now, he had headed up the main street towards the mountains. When he had come to where there were no more houses and the cars picked up speed for the open road, he'd veered into the bush and followed the water furrow. Within two hours, he had passed the braai spot and then the swimming hole, and was looking up at the twists and turns of the Swartberg Pass.

Leaving the road where he could take shortcuts between the hairpin bends, he had climbed, knowing that on the other side of the mountains it would be downhill to Oudtshoorn.

As the sun set over the peaks, he'd reached the first lookout point and his bare feet had been sore. For a while he'd sat with his feet in a stream that ran in a furrow next to the road, thinking about what he could eat. There were the remains of a tourist's picnic in the bin, and he had dusted off the ants and eaten the crusts and apple cores. He knew he was high up already, but still the road wound onwards and he wondered how long it would take to reach the top.

When night came, he'd crawled under an overhang to escape the breeze and, lying on his side, he'd rested his head on his hands with his knees pulled up to his chest. An engine idling had woken him, and he'd slithered from his hiding place to see who was on the road below. A bakkie's headlights lit up the track and he'd watched a big bony hare, its eyes shining red from the light, disappear into the veld. The engine had stopped and the lights had gone out. He heard two men scuffling and talking, and then he smelt cigarette smoke. As his eyes grew used to the dark, he saw their shapes looking out at the grey-black valley below. The burning ends of their cigarettes moved up and down, and he thought about Majola and the karretjieman who had smoked the cigarettes they had found in the dead Baas Jan's pocket. Boetie stood up slowly. *I am a snake*, he'd thought. *I am a snake moving like a shadow in the dark.*

When he'd reached the bakkie, he had seen it was loaded with tools, bedding rolls, and sacks of cement. By the time he heard the men grind their stompies under their heels, laughing and talking, he was wedged between the sacks and their bedding. The engine started and the bakkie pulled back onto the road, but he did not move. It was only when it wound upwards, slowing on the bends and then accelerating on the straights, that he exhaled and stretched out his legs.

The driver had battled down the Oudtshoorn side of the

pass. The melting snow had carved gullies in the road that were impossible to see in the dark, and several times the vehicle had lurched so that Boetie's head hit against the tools above him. To stop from sliding, he'd braced his feet against the tailgate and his shoulders against the cement, but even then, he had been thrown from side to side. The vibrations of the vehicle on the rutted track had made his head buzz and, by the time it reached the tarmac, he'd felt bruised, his teeth aching from the rattling. When it picked up speed, he lay on his back and watched the stars. He had been aware of distance passing, but was afraid to sit up. Only when the street lights of Oudtshoorn had appeared above him was he sure they had arrived, and that it was time to get off. The vehicle paused at a traffic light and he lifted his head but, before he could leap out, it was on the move again. On the outskirts of town, it swung into a petrol station and he heard the doors slam as the men headed for the all-night café. They were laughing and talking, and he heard a petrol attendant call after them, saying they should fill up because the road to George was far and there was nowhere else for diesel. When they'd returned, sipping early morning coffee from paper cups and carrying vetkoek in paper bags, Boetie was gone.

Finding the jail had been easy. A domestic worker walking to her char job had pointed him in the right direction. Boetie had watched the wardens arrive for work and groups of uniformed children carrying heavy book bags pass on their way to school. When the street had quietened, he'd crossed over and stood in front of the solid doors, thinking he should knock as he had in the town he had left behind, but this time he was afraid. He didn't know this place or recognise any of the faces passing in the streets. He glanced at the distant peaks that made a long solid black line on the horizon. He had crossed them, and now town and the valley were faraway and he couldn't go back. He knew no one – except Ou Ana – in this place. He was very hungry and very lonely. Tears welled in his tired eyes, and he sat on the prison's steps, covering his face with his arm to hide the sobs that rumbled through him like thunder.

A police van stopped at the side of the prison, and its driver climbed out and opened the gate. When he saw Boetie, the policeman shouted: 'Hey, what do you want?'

Boetie looked up and wiped his face on his T-shirt. 'Policeman, please, I want Ou Ana. She is inside, in the jail.'

'If this Ou Ana is in here, you must forget about her. It means she is rubbish. Now voetsak. Go.'

Boetie felt so weary he didn't argue but stood up, careful to keep his eyes down, and walked away. He crossed the road further up and, when at last he looked back, he saw the policeman had pulled the van inside and the gate was closed. He sat on the kerb watching the entrance. The warden in town had said Ou Ana was here. One day she had to come out for court. All he had to do was wait at the gate.

In the late afternoon, his hunger forced him onto his feet, and he took a side street to the river where he had walked at dawn. He came to a strip mall, and for a while ferreted through bins at the back door of a restaurant, eating pizza crusts that had been scrapped off plates. Eventually he made his way round, into a parking lot. A woman let him push her grocery trolley to her car and gave him a coin.

'For food, not glue – you hear!' she said, which he thought was a strange thing to say. He would have pushed more trolleys, but a car guard chased him with a sjambok. The money was enough for two slices of bread and a boiled egg from a street trader, and he drank water from the tap in the public toilet at the petrol station where he had jumped off the bakkie just twelve hours earlier. After he had eaten, he felt less tearful, and made his way back to the prison. In less than one day, he had come to Oudtshoorn, found the prison, and earned money. And he already knew his way around. For the first time since the day the police had taken Ou Ana and Majola away, he felt hope.

That night, and for many after that, he slept under a bush, behind the jail, against a wall. Ou Ana was inside and he was outside and, although he couldn't see her, he sensed she was close. He fell asleep to the prisoners' singing, and awoke to the smell of their breakfast cooking. He didn't call to her again, but every day he learnt the routine on the other side of the wall. Eating, cleaning, washing, talking, singing, eating, sleeping. Sometimes laughing. Sometimes fighting. Sometimes crying. The prisoners were moved all the time – taken and brought back, and some even released. Two afternoons a week, visitors, carrying bags of chips and cooldrinks, queued outside. He wanted to join the line but he was afraid. He knew he was dirty and hungry, and he didn't want them to call welfare and take him back to the house on the N1. Instead, he stayed hidden and watched for them to bring Ou Ana out to be taken to court. Days passed, but he never saw her face among those peering from the grill at the back of the police van, even when he went up close enough for the prisoners to call out to him.

Boetie had been sleeping beside the jail wall for many nights when he thought of Siena again. It happened on one of his better days, when he had made enough money to eat and hadn't been chased. The guard with the sjambok was sick and Boetie had pushed trolleys all day, smiling big smiles at ladies who gave him two rand for taking their trolleys back to the shop. In privacy, under his bush, he counted his money. There was enough for hot chips, a half-loaf, a Sparberry, and some change. Maybe he should rather have a sausage or fried fish, he thought. No, no … that would cost too much. He would buy chips. He went to a café close to the jail to avoid the street children in the town centre who would steal his cash. The hot chips were wrapped in white paper and their oily-vinegar smell almost drove him mad with hunger as he carried the package back to his bush. Eyes closed, he chewed slowly, finishing his meal with the Sparberry and a long burp. The remaining coins he buried under his sleeping place and settled in, out of sight of the main road, to play a game with stones that Majola had taught him. It was then that Siena came, unexpectedly but very clearly, into his mind.

'Siena?' he said aloud. 'Where have you been?'

Her smile became a laugh and he reached out as if to take her hand.

The last time he had seen her, she had been sitting next to the mevrou in the front of the white bakkie on her way back to school in Seekoegat. Everyone in the valley knew Siena had been sent away because she and Boetie had killed the tortoise. That day, he had waited at the roadside, near the workers' shacks, to watch them leave. When the bakkie had passed, he'd waved, but when Siena went to school, she always stared straight ahead.

No one said he should be sent to school in Seekoegat but, even if they had, he knew he wouldn't have stayed there. Teachers, with their shouting and their hitting and making him sit still all day writing in books, weren't for him. What he wanted was for Majola and Ou Ana to come back, even though they never had bread. He wanted to smell the Karoo doringhout burn on the night fire that Majola lit when the sun set. He wanted to eat whatever meat Majola had snared, and then he wanted to crawl under their blanket, between them, to sleep, listening to the jackals and feeling Ou Ana's rough hands rubbing his back.

Siena could read and write by now and, once a person could do that, they weren't the same any more, he thought. She would sit in front at church wearing shiny shoes with long socks and have ribbons in her hair. Maybe she'd say things like, 'I'll read this,' or, 'I'll write that.' The old Siena, with her kind face, was dead by now. For sure, he really was all alone.

Boetie remembered that, after the tortoise incident, the mevrou had called the karretjieman to the big house. Her eyes had been wild and Boetie had seen that even the karretjieman was afraid. From his hiding place in the branches of the big shade tree, he'd heard the mevrou say, 'These children are out of control,' and then: 'They must go to school.' The karretjieman had nodded and said, 'Ja, the mevrou is right.' The very next day she had told them both to get on the bakkie, and they went into town, straight to the primary school.

'Mevrou,' the headmaster had said, 'you know I need their birth certificates.'

'Yes, yes,' she'd said, 'I will sort that out. But this is urgent.'

'How old are they?' he'd asked.

'The girl is eight, and the boy about nine or ten.'

'About nine or ten?'

'Nine. He is nine.'

'We can't take him in grade one. He is too big. He has missed his chance.'

'He is nine, and he needs to be in grade one.'

The headmaster had looked reluctantly at Siena and Boetie. Boetie had known straight away that school, for him, wasn't going to happen.

'Why don't we send them to Seekoegat Primary?' the headmaster had said.

'Seekoegat? But that is so faraway.'

'It's a perfect place for children like these,' the headmaster had said. 'They need to learn the basics, Mevrou – how to wash, clean their teeth, use a lavatory.' He'd looked at the two of them who had been told to sit at the mevrou's feet. Siena was tearful, while Boetie was bored and, having moved onto his stomach, was slithering under the headmaster's desk. 'It is quite obvious these children are off the cart and have never been taught to sit still and listen.'

So it had been decided. Siena would go to Seekoegat Primary. Boetie, lying on his stomach, studying the head-master's scuffed brown shoes, heard that the welfare man should be called to deal with him. He had become the me-vrou's problem and, really, he was a problem she didn't want. Whatever happened, he'd known he would up and leave if he didn't like it. It was what Majola had taught him. 'If a boer becomes demanding and you don't like it on the farm any more, then go. It's all people like us have – the freedom to go.'

When the welfare man eventually had come, it was to take Boetie to his people on the N1. He had been left with an aunt who, the welfare man had said, was Boetie's mother's sister. Boetie had looked at her with suspicion. She was not Ou Ana's sister, that he'd known for sure. This one was much too young. There were six children in the yard watching when the welfare man's car had pulled up. Once the paperwork had been signed and he'd driven away, they'd crowded around Boetie, pinching and pushing him. The aunt, who had been given money and promised more to keep Boetie, had wan-dered down the road to the shebeen. Boetie never went into the small redbrick house. He'd turned, looked at the distant Swartberg and, without a word to the other children who were still prodding him and laughing, he had walked out the gate. He never took his eyes off the mountains as he crossed the N1, skirted around the Shell garage, and headed into the veld. Maybe he could go back to Baas Jan's farm and live in the hok, he thought. He could stay there until Majola and

Ou Ana came back, and then they could decide together what they would do next.

Now, as he lay under the bush next to the Oudtshoorn prison with his back against the wall, he smiled when he remembered those days. He had come so far and made his own money. The welfare man would never catch him now, and he planned to sit it out waiting for Ou Ana to be freed. But thinking about Siena changed things. He was bored waiting outside the jail. He wanted to play with somebody and run in the veld and catch crabs and eat birds' eggs. If he found a tortoise, then so what … The mevrou was faraway in the valley. He stood up and stretched, looking around with fresh eyes.

Chapter 9

NOW

Siena knew it was still a long way to Seekoegat and she had no idea where she was on the road. In the first hours after she had run away, familiar landmarks had passed unnoticed. Now, as she walked into the deepest part of the night, she strained to make out the landscape, hoping to recognise the outline of the mountains or the shape of the rocks. There was a koppie, as flat as a table, about twenty minutes in the back seat of the welfare man's car from town. Halfway was a broken windmill, its spokes pitted by some man with a gun. If she could find these landmarks, she would know how far she had come. And she knew, from the days with Pa and Ma on the karretjie, that there were places to find water.

Her mouth was dry and she was hungry. Soon she would need to drink, or thirst would crawl up her legs, move along her arms, and squeeze her heart. Pa had said a thirsty person could smell water on the breeze. Siena stopped, lifting her face to sniff, but there was just the faint metallic scent of blood. She flattened her palm over her heart, expecting to feel it pounding, but the steady rise and fall of her chest made her calmer, and so she breathed in more deeply and blew out through her mouth. She was a woman on a road in the night. The boere had no right to stop and question her and, if the police came – as she knew they would – she would hide like she had when she was little. But no one came, and all she could do was walk, thinking of Aunt Esme and saying sorry to God.

'Dear God?'

Her voice startled her and she coughed to reassure herself.

'Forgive me, please forgive me … God, you really must be the moer-in with me. I don't blame you. You make a person and then someone else, like me, comes along and, zip-zap, they kill them. But, really, he was a bastard, God. You must have been looking after people in Cape Town, God, because, really, if you knew what went on in our hok, you would have done something about it. God, it's better he is gone, for Ma and Sussie and … and … for me. Put me in jail, God. I don't care. It's finish and klaar now. I know that.' She looked to the heavens as she spoke, as if she expected a giant hand to reach down and give her a shove.

The image of his severed throat, with its bubbling hot blood, charged into her mind. His dying lips had parted in a smile. Siena never had been able tell what he was thinking, and he was always thinking. She crossed her hands, one over the other, on her chest again as her breaths came in gasps. He was dead. It was over.

'Oh, God, please … help me … I am sorry.'

Other than the one bakkie, there had been no other passing vehicles for several hours. Tiredness flooded through her; she thought she should sleep in the veld. Pa had outspanned in small clearings next to the road. He'd sit on his Frisco tin next to their small fire, tapping his foot as he played the mouth organ, stopping to talk to Ma about something they had seen in the day. The donkeys never wandered far but kept close to the camp, tugging at the hard grey leaves of dusty bushes, snorting and stamping. Siena had fallen asleep to those sounds, never worrying about scorpions and snakes or police. Ah, really,

God wasn't joking when he'd filled the world with creatures and men that stung and stabbed and bit and beat you. None of it mattered now. If she lay down with a scorpion or a snake, then this life and this pain would be done with. Sooner or later the police would find her, but, until they did, she would carry on to Seekoegat. If she made it, then she would have Aunt Esme and Meneer Maans, who would know what to do.

When she'd left the hok, all those hours ago, after his blood had sprayed the walls, there had been no thought of taking anything. Now, she wished she had sloppies for the stones and her tracksuit top to cover her kitchen clothes, covered with gravy stains and scabs of his dry blood that she had been picking at while she walked. She remembered that Sussie had stood up from the table as his head had fallen back, and she'd thought the girl was laughing. Had Sussie laughed as he gasped and gurgled, or was that laughing before he came in the hok, when Sussie had been tickling her while they were lying on the mattress? Siena couldn't remember. Blood then laughter, or laugher then blood. She shook her head, but Sussie's laughing face kept swimming around in blood.

'Sussie, go sleep, asseblief. Stop laughing, this is a terrible business. Gaan!'

Ma must have come home by now and, if she wasn't too drunk, she might clean up the blood and the messed food; and someone would have fetched the police. The ambulance would take his body, and then the police would look for her. Sussie would hide in the shadows, watching and, when everyone was gone and the place cleaned up, she would creep inside to sleep in the bed Siena had made for her in the corner on the floor. *God, please let there not be blood on Sussie's pink comforter.*

'It's okay, Sus, really you must sleep now. Enough is enough.'

No, no! Don't talk to her, she is not here. Siena shook her head to clear her mind.

There were nightjars on the track, and their chirruping and fluttering made the staggering loneliness recede. Occasionally, she sensed other life as a hare or black-backed jackal darted from her path into the scrub. It was at that time of night when the stars were closest that she knew Pa was walking with her again. The mists of the Milky Way made her light-headed and, when she looked at the pointers of the Southern Cross, she remembered how he had told her they were the eyes of her dead ancestors looking down on her, that they had been there since the beginning of the world.

'They are watching over us, my Sienatjie. They know about every day of our suffering.'

'They are stars, Pa.'

'Beautiful souls, Sienatjie, watching over us.'

'No, Pa. Just stars.'

'God made us and he made them. We don't understand the mystery of what is in the sky.'

'Ag nee, God is just this person who people made up. If there really was a God, I wouldn't be running down a road like a mal mens after cutting open a man's throat.'

'Dear God, please give Siena food to eat and school shoes.'

'I slaughtered him like a sheep, Pa. And I don't need school shoes – I am done with school.'

'Dear God, please give Siena All Stars.'

'Actually, could you rather say, "Dear God, please give Siena a head start on the police."'

'Sienatjie, I should never have let the mevrou send you away.'

'No, Pa, it was the best thing that happened to me.'

They walked in silence for a while and then she said: 'You know, Pa, to hold a pen, like a learned person, is a feeling that gives you power … When you see a book on a teacher's desk and realise you understand the words written on its cover, it makes you feel very important. I loved school, Pa. I loved the smell of my teacher who bathed every day and wore spray. I loved her smile when I tried hard. I loved Aunt Esme in the kitchen, and that she worried if I didn't eat breakfast. Can you imagine, Pa? We ate breakfast, lunch, and supper every day. Some days I wasn't even hungry. Pa, can you believe it? Me, Siena, sometimes didn't feel hungry.'

'Ja, no wonder you got so fat.'

'I wasn't fat – that's what a child looks like when she is not starving.'

Pa started humming a tune she knew from his playing on his mouth organ and she smiled and joined in.

When he stopped, he said: 'And now? It will have been all for nothing after this. What's going to happen to you?'

'They will put me in jail. That is what I deserve. If that doesn't happen, then I am going to become like Ma, searching for a drink and a smoke to take away the pain.'

'What pain did Ma have?'

'Ag, Pa. Voetsak now. Asseblief. Please.'

'Why are you walking along this road by yourself? You should be with Ma. Who is looking after Ma and her pain with you out here?'

'You drank and Ma drank. It was always about a papsak for the two of you. You did it because your life was miserable, and Ma did it because hers was meaningless. You know that.'

'Ja, but Ma never thought about cutting her man's throat. Lucky for me! And why did you take that rubbish man in in the first place. He was a no good skelm – you knew that.'

'Luister, Pa, if you are going to walk with me, then don't talk to me like you are one of the church boeties. You have no right to do that because you never set foot in a church and I really don't feel like all your judging. Please!'

'You never blerrie listened. Your ma was always standing in my way when I wanted to take the belt to you. I should have klapped you instead of her.'

'And now you ask me why she has pain. Phew!'

'I never gave my old father any trouble and he moered me all the time. It was because of him I was working on the farm before my big teeth were out. I was strong because of him.'

'Pa, you spent your whole life searching for hidden-away dagga plants so you could roll pynpille.'

'I had my aches and sorrows. Working day and night. Those pille gave me happiness in a bitter life. Why are you so full of kak about all this now?'

'Go now, Pa. I want to walk in peace and quiet.'

She stopped and turned to make her point again, but he was gone. Only the sweetness of his dagga smoke hung on the breeze. 'Ag, Pa,' she whispered, 'I didn't really want you to go ...'

Siena thought about what Aunt Esme would say about what she had done. If the aunt chased her away, she would beg for clothes and shoes from the farms, and maybe hitch-hike to Beaufort West. No one would know her in Beaufort; she could try for a domestic job. Maybe some mevrou would take a shine to her because she could read and write. She didn't steal or drink, but a mevrou wouldn't know that. A girl like her could clean lavatories and stay out of trouble. Nobody need ever know that she had sliced open a man with broken glass. There were also the trucks. Blommie, one of the karre-tjie girls from long ago, had ridden the trucks after her Pa had sold his donkeys. That girl had made good money on the trucks, and bought Fanta and cigarettes every day until she got sick. That karretjiemeid, Blommie, with her soft voice and half smile, was dead now.

When a red line appeared on the horizon, Siena climbed through the fence and walked into the veld looking for a gwarriebos where she could sleep in the shade, and which would hide her from anyone passing by. When she found one, she threw stones underneath to disturb any puff adders already asleep underneath. There were no crescent-shaped scorpion burrows, nor little grass mouse nests, so she went down on her hands and knees and crawled in under the low spikey branches. When the blood-sun rose, she was asleep. Pa was with her again, except this time she was sitting next to him on the step of a labourer's cottage and he was making her a toy karretjie for her aspop, Maaitjie, the one Ma had made from sack, filled with ash and fastened with baling twine. They were on a farm somewhere on the plains because she could see the Swartberg faraway. Ma was singing and turning roosterkoek on stones nestled between the coals in the evening fire.

Siena awoke in the late afternoon. Several vehicles had passed during the day, but she had slept despite them. The road was quiet and she stood, looking around, her mind again on water. There was a windmill in the far distance and she crossed the road heading towards it, thinking it would probably be dry, as most of the boere used sun pumps now. As she drew closer, she picked up the criss-cross of sheep spoor in the sand and knew she was in luck. Two sparrows were playing under a drip between the pump and the dam, and they fluttered off when she approached. The water was brackish but she drank, wrinkling her nose and thinking that surely no sheep was ever as desperate. It was a chance to wash the blood off her clothes, and she climbed onto the dam wall, lowering herself in. It was cold, but she sank onto her haunches, letting the brown water cover her shoulders and feeling the mud between her toes while she watched the muggies dance in the afternoon sun. She floated on her back, squinting in the glare of the white-blue sky. There were no clouds, just the endless heavens. A dragonfly touched the water near her, its wings clicking like electricity, before it lifted off, and she wondered if the sparrows would eat it.

She hoisted herself onto the dam wall, sitting on the edge to dry off. A small flock of ewes watched her, waiting for her to go so they could come to their trough. She thought about slaughtering one and her stomach squeezed at the idea of meat, but she knew she didn't have the strength to run one down, nor did she have a knife or matches and wood for a fire. A yellow tsamma melon on a vine under the windmill caught her eye, and her relief was so overwhelming that she laughed and the ewes moved away. The melon was ripe and it cracked easily. She swallowed its bitter flesh quickly, not even spitting the seeds out. It was the first time she had eaten since she had been on the run, and she felt suddenly stronger and less hopeless. A karretjiemeid would not die in the veld. Even though her teacher had taught her to read and write, those things Ma and Pa had done without thinking – those things they had learnt from their mas and pas – she knew too. She squatted on her haunches and scanned the landscape as she ate. When she saw nothing that interested her, she climbed to the platform under the head of the windmill and studied the veld some more.

Siena saw the police car stop. A policeman in his blue uniform climbed out and looked at the soft sand at the side of the road. When she had cut in to the windmill, she had kept to the hard ground, knowing that, unless they thought about her thirst, they would keep looking for her along the road. The policeman climbed back into the car and drove off, disappearing between the koppies.

'They are looking for you,' Pa said, nodding at the road. He was sitting beside her on their high perch and had been swinging his legs, watching the sheep until the police car had stopped.

Siena said nothing. She was watching the horizon, and turned suddenly to climb down.

'Where are you going now?' he said.

A smile crept into her eyes.

'Seekoegat, Pa. The police are in front of me now, so at least I can stop looking back.'

Chapter 10

BEFORE

The plastic bottle Boetie clutched to his chest held the faint smell of petrol. His legs were splayed and stretched so that his bare feet were off the kerb protruding into the intersection. His face, criss-crossed with little scars from crawling under the bush at the jail, was burnt dark, and his lips were blistered from sunburn and petrol. Some drivers glanced at him when they stopped at the red light, and one or two pedestrians prodded him with a foot and said, 'Hey.' When he stirred, and they saw he was alive, they walked on.

The bell rang at the primary school a block away. Rolling onto his side, he opened his eyes. He needed to move before the children came out or else the boys would kick him around like a ball. Last time he had been so bruised, it had taken days before he could walk without pain. His lips closed around the mouth of the bottle, and he sucked in hard so that the rush of fumes burnt his chest and his brain dulled.

The intersection was a good place to beg. Sometimes he made twenty rand in a morning but today, after Sam had put some petrol in his bottle, Boetie had had no motivation to dodge cars or face insults from drivers. He had planned to sit on the kerb only for a little while, but, when he did that, he'd inevitably drifted off. He should have known it would happen again.

He was hot and thirsty and, when he sat up, his eyes swollen and blurry, children were already streaming out the school gate. He stood, stumbling slightly, and walked up the road, back to the petrol station. Sam was on day shift this week and would let him use the tap. He always did.

'Jirre, Boeta, you look like shit,' Sam said. 'You need a bath, and to stop with these petrol bottles. You are looking like a skebenga. People are going to run a mile when you get close.'

'I am thirsty,' Boetie said.

'Okay, you know where's the tap. When I get a chance, I'll get you ietsie to eat. Jirre, ou maat, what are we going to do with you?'

Boetie went to the tap outside the public toilets and drank. The water was warm, and he put his head under the stream and rubbed his face. The toilets were always locked and for customers only, so he went behind the building and peed against the wall. When Boetie came back, the water glistening on his hair, Sam was filling up a car, and he sat down in the shade at the edge of the forecourt and watched him. After a while, he fell asleep again.

'Boeta, boeta, come, wake up, here's your ietsie. Open your eyes and eat because if the boss comes and sees me encouraging you here, it will be the sjambok for both of us. Wake up, now.' Sam put a mug of Coke on the ground next to him with a chunk of bread balancing on top. 'Joh … ou maat! This petrol sniffing is going to kill you,' he said again.

The Coke was cold and the gas burnt Boetie's raw throat, but the relief from the sweetness almost made him cry. He broke a small piece off the bread and, rolling it into a ball, he placed it on his tongue and sucked it. The food and Sam's fussing eased the throbbing inside him, and, when at last the bread was finished, he slept again.

When Boetie awoke, it was late afternoon. He studied the

faces on the forecourt and, when he saw Sam on his haunches pumping a car's tyres, he lay down and put his hands under his head.

'Boeta, you were lucky today. I heard the boss went to Mossel Bay, but he will be back here any minute to change the shift. You need to move, sorry, my ou maat.'

Boetie sat up. It had been one of those days when he couldn't stay awake and he still felt dull and tired.

He crossed the road to the vacant plot, looking for a place where he could suck on his petrol bottle and pass out again. He would slip back to his bush at the jail after dark. It had been so long already and no one had found him there; he knew it was because he kept his comings and goings to the shadows.

Some nights now he didn't go back to the jail, and instead walked up the hill to the lokasie. It was here that he could escape the loneliness that followed him. On Friday nights, he joined the dancing in the streets outside the taverns, scoring polystyrene cups of wine when the men on wages were drunk and buying for everyone. There was always work the next day when the tavern owner needed a handlanger to pick up the bottles, sweep the broken glass, and hose off the vomit in the yard. For his effort, Boetie could make ten rand.

The lokasie was where, on a washing line, he found his first long pants; and, last winter, he had slipped through an open door and found a blue labourer's jacket over the back of a chair. There had been a wallet in the pocket with twenty rand mixed in with cash slips. For a few days, he had worn the jacket like a working man, checking through the slips and their strange numbers like someone who goes to the shops for his family. When he'd grown tired of the game, he'd kicked the wallet into a storm water drain and used the twenty rand for bread and chips.

Now, after he had crossed the road, Boetie saw three boys sitting against the fence on the far side of the vacant plot, passing a cigarette rolled from newspaper back and forth. A dagga smell hung on the evening air, and he felt a pang of nostalgia for Majola who had also enjoyed a skyf at this time. Boetie pretended to ignore the boys, but sat where he could see them, keeping his face hidden.

One of them stood and looked at him. As he walked, he rolled his shoulders, as if he were a gangster, but Boetie could see he was just a street child. His red t-shirt was stretched across his chest, exposing his stomach, and his grey tracksuit pants were torn and dirty. He had takkies, though, without laces, but still, his feet were covered. Boetie tucked his legs up so that he was completely in the shadow. He was sorry now that he had come here. He knew street children liked this place and he wouldn't be left alone. The boy was standing over him now and nudged him with a toe.

'Give me that bottle.'

Boetie raised his head and met the boy's stare, which was blank and hard.

'Leave me alone.'

'Hey, you whore's child, give me the bottle.'

The street lights came on and Boetie looked over at the other two, still sitting against the far fence, their eyes glinting in the yellow-green light.

The boy grabbed at the bottle, but Boetie was ready and rolled to the side, and the boy stumbled forwards onto his hands and knees. Boetie's sluggishness was gone; he was on his feet. He used his heel on the boy's buttocks to unbalance him and he fell flat again. As the boy tried to stand, Boetie rounded on him, stamping on him and then kicking at his face. The boy's nose was bleeding and he gasped to regain his wind. When Boetie came at him again, the boy grabbed his foot, and he went down. The boy was on top of him and, like feral cats, they screamed and rolled in the dirt, biting and scratching, until Boetie sensed the other boys circling too. One of them shouted, 'Pikka, hier's vir jou 'n blade!' They were on their backsides, panting and scrabbling onto their haunches. The boy smiled through his blood as he moved the knife into position. But Boetie had Majola's small knife and, even with its handmade wire handle, it was sharp and familiar. He too was ready to strike.

Blood streamed into his mouth, and he spat it into the other boy's face, kicking at his legs. They went down again, stabbing and missing, until Boetie rolled on top, gripping the boy's wrists and trying to hold on to his slither of steel. The other two kicked at Boetie, but many of their blows connected with their friend. Boetie leant down and bit into the boy's armpit. As he screamed and bucked, his knife – a strong black-handled kitchen knife – fell into the sand and Boetie released his grip. There was no circling or dodging, just one hard thrust as he felt Majola's thin blade pierce the boy's exposed stomach. There was a small rush of gas, like a deflating balloon, and the boy moaned and fell back. The street lights, glowing gold now, lit up the surprise on the boy's bloodied face. Boetie saw his mouth moving and, as life left him, he heard him say, 'Mamma ...'

'You killed him ... You killed Pikka!' they were shouting. The dead boy stank of shit and blood, and Boetie vomited where he sat, next to the body. A cut on his face ached and he touched it with a finger.

The boys were on the ground slapping at their friend's face. Blood was pooling in the sand, and Boetie crawled towards them, pushing them apart to pull his knife from the boy's stomach. He was on his feet in an instant, poised for attack again.

'Who else wants to die? Hey. Who wants to die tonight?'

In their eyes was little boys' fear, and they backed away and ran. He was alone with the dead boy then, and he cleaned the blood off his knife with a handful of soil, slipping it – and the forgotten kitchen knife – into the pocket of his blood-covered blue jacket.

He felt nothing for the dead boy. Instead, there was a hardening within Boetie and, when he walked away, he didn't look back. He went to his washing place in the river and packed black mud onto his wounds, before making his way back to the jail, where he crawled deep under his bush. More than anything he wanted to sleep, but his face throbbed. He heard the familiar hum of voices on the other side of the wall as the prisoners washed the supper pots. When he fell asleep, he dreamt he was swimming with Siena and she was shouting for him to be careful, that the mermaid would grab his ankles and pull him under. Several times in the night he awoke when he felt the mermaid's firm cold hands grab at his feet, and each time he took deep gulps of air.

He stayed under the bush all of the next day and night. Sleeping, then watching, and sleeping again. On the second morning, he couldn't ignore the pain or his thirst, and before sunrise he went back to the river. He walked upstream for a way, until he was in the thick reeds. The water was cleaner there, and he drank and washed more dried blood off his arms and face. He took off his blue jacket and pants and rubbed mud into the stains, then hung them to dry on the reeds. For most of the day he sat on a hidden rock, swatting at the flies that settled on the cut. He needed food and something for the cut. Before the street lights came on again, he had slipped back into his sun-stiffened clothes and was on his way to the lokasie.

It was early evening, and the smells of pots on stoves bubbled over into the streets. Children were playing in the twilight, their mothers starting to call for them to come home.

He waited until the lokasie settled, and then knocked on a door where he knew an old couple lived alone.

'Ouma, I have hurt my face, please … Ouma, can you help me?'

The old woman was in her gown, her hair released from its daytime doek and her feet bare. She hesitated to open the door, but when she saw he was bleeding she pushed her feet into her blue slippers and stepped outside.

'That looks bad, like a bite. You must go to the hospital for stitches.'

'Ag, Ouma, help me.' He was Boetie, the charming one.

She muttered, turning away from him to the open door, and he sat on the step until she came back with a bottle of mercurochrome and a roll of plaster.

'Come on, come sit in the light.' She cleaned the wound and closed it with a length of plaster.

'It's not too bad – you are lucky,' she said. 'Don't put mud in it again. Mud is old people's medicine.' They both laughed.

'Ag dankie, my ouma, ag dankie.' He remembered to be obsequious; Ou Ana and Majola had been good at that.

The old woman gave him tea and bread, and then quietly closed the door, and he heard the lock turn. When he was finished eating, he used the outhouse and settled to sleep beneath their bedroom window. He had slept there before. He liked listening to the ouma cough. She always did that when she prepared for bed. And then there was the murmur of the old man's voice as he read aloud from the Bible. Boetie tried to stay awake until they switched off their light, but he was asleep before the Bible reading was finished.

In the early hours, he stirred. His face felt better and he sat up. He needed different clothes, and he wandered through the streets looking for washing left on a line. It didn't take long. When he left the lokasie, he had on grey school pants and a green T-shirt. His old clothes he bundled in a ball and dropped into a toilet pit. He kept the blue jacket because he liked the pockets.

When the sun rose, he was sitting outside the tavern where he sometimes worked. The man who ran the place was always early and, when he came out to load the previous night's empties on his bakkie, Boetie was ready.

'I want a job,' he said. 'I want a job so I can buy shoes.'

The man laughed. 'You are a skebenga – why must I give you a job?'

'I want to work.'

'Okay, Skebenga, load these crates on the bakkie. Let's see how you work today.'

Boetie loaded the bakkie and, within the hour, he and the man were on their way to the next shebeen to pick up more empties. At the end of the day he gave Boetie thirty rand.

'Laaitie, you can come tomorrow. If you work like you did today, then I can give you a job. If you drink or steal, I will bliksem you so that you will be brain damaged. Understand?'

Boetie nodded. He wanted takkies and now he had thirty rand. As the tavern man walked away, Boetie thought about how long it would take before this man pushed him too far. Then he would bliksem the tavern man until *he* was brain damaged.

Chapter 11

NOW

The road dipped and curved through a cluster of koppies that, at last, broke the shimmering monotony of the veld. The sky was cloudless and Siena was grateful for the giant rocks and the chance of shade under an overhang where she could rest. There might be water too, she thought. She felt she had been here before; the rocks gave her a sense of relief and peace, and she wondered if they had stopped here with the karretjie.

Donkeys could smell water and, when they veered off the track, tossing their defeated heads and stamping their worn hooves, Pa had known there was a spring. He would unhitch the karretjie and let them wander, noses to the ground, while she and Ma made camp. The donkeys always found the spring quickly, and Pa left them to drink and roll and pull at the dry grass growing between the boulders.

Afterwards, when they were all sated, Pa would touch their backs and rub their ears. 'Dankie, my ou Pienkie, dankie, my ou Haas,' he'd say. 'My old girls, you found us water again.'

So many times, when Siena had thought they would die of thirst, Pienkie and Haas had smelt out water.

'Close your eyes and use your nose – be like the donkeys,' a voice said.

Siena's heart skipped a beat. She had seen no one on her

approach but now, sitting flat on the ground in the shadow of an overhang, was an old woman, barefoot and smoking a pipe.

'Ouma Loos?'

The old woman giggled, covering her toothless gums with the back of her free hand. The skin around her eyes and mouth was pinched, as if she had spent her life laughing. Her threadbare dress, pale blue and dusted with small pink roses, hung off her shoulders so that when she moved she exposed tiny, sun-wrinkled breasts. A frayed white doek was loosely tied on her head.

'What is Ouma Loos doing here? This is the middle of nowhere.'

'I know this place, my child,' Ouma Loos said, giggling again.

Not wanting to leave her, Siena sat on a rock next to the old woman, who looked at her with milky eyes. She seemed so happy that Siena smiled too, and the desolation that had chased her along the road rose and moved off.

'My jinne, my child, but you are so big now,' the old woman said.

'Ja, Ouma Loos, I have grown up. And you, Ouma? You are just the same. Where have you been, Ouma?'

The old woman ignored the question, but turned back to her pipe, prodding the tobacco in its bowl with a match. She had a box of matches on her lap and, when she was satisfied she had the tobacco right, she lit the pipe and sucked hard. Exhaling, she sighed and leant back against the rock.

'Ai, dis nou lekker, my kind!' she said.

Seeing the old lady made Siena think of the dark nights singing and dancing and stamping with cousins and uncles and aunts in the outspan.

'You have 'n trekkie now,' Ouma Loos said, offering the

pipe. Siena took it and put its mouthpiece, wet from Ouma Loos's sucking, between her lips and tried to inhale.

'I don't know how to smoke a pipe,' Siena said. 'I got nothing.'

'Make a kiss, like this.' Ouma Loos pursed her lips and, with loud smacking noises, she kissed the air and they both laughed. 'Okay, now close your lips and pull, like you do with a cigarette.'

Siena sucked and coughed.

'There we go – dit was nou mooi!'

Ouma Loos took the pipe back and, touching the tobacco lightly with her thumb to make sure it was burning, she took another drag.

'Like so.' She pursed her lips and took an exaggerated pull before passing the pipe back to Siena.

They smoked in silence until the tobacco was finished, and then Ouma Loos gently knocked out the ashes against the rock where Siena was sitting.

'Ouma Loos, when did I last see you? I can't remember,' Siena said. 'Aitog, Ouma Loos, I forgot all about you and the aunties and uncles … Maybe it was because of all those years I was at school.'

'Ja, my child, school can make a person forget the important things,' Ouma Loos said. 'Where is your Ma these days?'

'She is in town, in the lokasie. We have a hok there.'

The old woman said nothing, but wiggled her toes, then scratched a mosquito bite on one leg.

'She takes a dop, you know, Ouma.'

Ouma Loos nodded.

'And Pa is dead now … from the TB.'

'Ah, that's a pity. I am sorry to hear that. The TB took Oupa Tok too.' The old woman started coughing, holding on to Siena's arm as she tried to catch her breath. When it was over, she spat a glob of bloody phlegm at a rock a little way off, and Siena wondered if the TB wasn't also in Ouma Loos's chest.

The sun had moved over the koppie. Siena helped the old woman to her feet, and they found a spot deeper in the shade where they sat again.

'Look, look there – see what is hiding.' Ouma Loos giggled and pointed her pipe at a tortoise who had pushed under a granaatbos. 'It's telling us today is going to be hot. See, it also wants shade.'

A wave of nausea swept over Siena, and she turned and retched but, because she hadn't eaten anything except the tsamma melon hours earlier, nothing came out. Ouma Loos ignored her, reaching over to stroke the tortoise's rippled shell.

'I like to eat a tortoise in the summer, not in the winter when they sleep – then the meat is too dry and tough,' Ouma Loos said. 'My old pa said there had to be one thing that the earth gave us that is easy to catch and eat – everything else is such a struggle.'

'Do you eat tortoise? My pa would never let us eat one,' Siena said.

'Your pa had a lot of funny ideas,' Ouma Loos said. 'When you are starving, you eat what the earth gives you.'

'I have killed a tortoise,' Siena said.

'Did you like the taste?'

'No, Ouma Loos, I didn't eat it. The mevrou made us have a funeral for it and say a prayer. I dug its grave.'

Ouma Loos looked at Siena in disbelief, her hand shooting to her mouth as she giggled again. 'That is a pity – they taste very nice.'

'Actually, that tortoise caused a lot of trouble.'

'Yes, if you kill one and don't eat it, there is always trouble. God doesn't like you to waste his gift,' said Ouma Loos.

Siena was tired from the talking, and she shifted onto the

ground, to Ouma Loos's feet, where she lay down. The old woman relit her tobacco and hummed softly as she smoked, so that Siena again felt the peace of the place settle over her and she fell asleep. The overhang stayed shaded for most of the day. When she awoke, the sun was low and red. Ouma Loos was gone, and she looked around to see if the old woman was sitting somewhere else, but there was no sign of her. The tortoise was still there. When it sensed her stirring, it pushed further under the granaatbos.

'Ag, tortoise, I am not going to do anything to you. Just relax,' she said aloud.

Siena closed her eyes again and, on a whisper of wind, she picked up a damp scent, like coming rain. Silence surged and crashed around her so that she thought she was going mad. Then came the bubbling of a spring. When she opened her eyes, there were swallows, small black arrows shooting across the dying blue sky and dropping from sight behind the rocks. She struggled to her feet and, sniffing the air like Pienkie and Haas, she followed the birds.

Ouma Loos was at the spring, her feet in the wet sand. When she saw Siena, she smiled and beckoned to her. There was a trickle from between the rocks which disappeared in the sand.

'This is sweet water,' Ouma Loos said. 'Come and drink – you must be very thirsty.'

Moss was growing under the rock but, other than that, there was nothing in the area that gave any indication of water. Siena saw there were bees too, landing on the rock and crawling to the water's edge to drink.

'Just look at them, we can have honey,' said the old woman.

'Really? Ouma Loos, will they have honey?' Siena was excited at the idea of the sweetness but the old woman looked at her in disgust.

She shook her head. 'Aitog, Siena, school didn't help you very much.'

The hive was between rocks close to the spring, and Ouma Loos instructed Siena to find twigs. When she was satisfied they had enough, she made a smoky fire at the mouth of the rocks and stepped back to let it burn.

'They are going to sting us, Ouma,' said Siena. 'They know what we are after; they will sting us.' She was afraid, and she wondered if she should just leave the old woman to this madness and carry on walking now that she had had water.

'Be patient. I have taken honey from this hive many times. These bees know me and they don't sting if you warn them what you are going to do. They are happy to share if you ask them.'

The old woman reached deep between the rocks and broke off a section of dripping comb, filled with tiny larvae, which she gave to Siena before going back for another piece for herself.

'Lekker honey with bushman's rice,' Ouma Loos said, smacking her lips, her eyes shining as they focused on the honeycomb packed thick with white larvae.

They sat at the spring to eat, licking their fingers. When they were finished, they washed their hands and faces, and drank again. The food had given Siena energy; she wanted to walk.

'Ouma Loos, where are you going?'

'I will come with you,' the old woman said.

'Can you walk so far? I am going to Seekoegat Primary.'

'I won't come the whole way, my child, but it will be nice to have someone to talk to on the road.'

They set off, with Siena supporting Ouma Loos's arm, walking slowly.

'The honey was very good, Ouma.'

'Yes, when I was a child that was our sweets – there was no such thing as a twenty cent for the shops.'

'Where were you a child, Ouma? Where was your place?'

'It was right here, my ou Sienatjie, always here.'

'So I have been here before. My pa must have stopped here with the donkeys. I thought I knew that spring.'

Ouma Loos chuckled and patted Siena's hand.

'Yes, these rocks were once a very big outspan. When the white people came, they stopped here with their oxen, and before them the Boesman climbed to the top of the rocks to spot game when they were hunting.'

'And us, Ouma Loos? Was it our place too?'

'It has always been our place. We come from the Boesman.'

'No, Ouma Loos, I am not like a Boesman. I am a coloured off a karretjie and then from the lokasie.'

For a while they didn't talk. A great yellow moon rose over the Swartberg, and they watched it climb and settle itself in the night sky.

'That's a hunting moon,' Ouma Loos said. 'When I was a child, my pa and the other men would chase down an eland on a night like tonight. He was one of those who still knew how to shoot with a bow and arrow.'

'O jinne, the boere couldn't have been too happy with him hunting their eland.'

'The eland were here, Siena, like us, and the tortoises, and the springbok. We were all here before everyone else. We all belonged to God. I told you, we are from the Boesman.'

Siena thought about how hard Pa had worked to snare a porcupine, and how long it took to get it clean. It would have been wonderful to have an eland or a kudu to eat, especially if you didn't have to worry about the boere catching you when you made a fire.

'What happened then, Ouma Loos? What happened to

your pa and the Boesman?' Her question felt unexpected, even Siena was surprised she had asked it. Maybe he had died, like all old people, of a sickness that couldn't be cured?

In the moonlight, Siena saw the laughter in Ouma Loos's face was gone, despair now written into the lines and crevices.

'Sorry, Ouma …'

Ouma Loos stopped walking and turned, putting her rough hands on each side of Siena's face. 'He was shot, Siena. They shot him, just like an eland.'

Ouma Loos wiped the tears welling in Siena's eyes with her black thumbs. The memory had exhausted the old woman, so they sat next to the road for her to light her pipe again.

'My old ma told us that, on the night he was shot, he had turned himself into an eland, so the animals wouldn't be afraid of him when he raised his bow and arrow. Maybe when they killed him they thought he was a buck.'

'What did you do, Ouma Loos? What did you do without a pa?'

'We walked to town and my old ma asked around for work. Eventually, she got something and we were taken to one of the farms. The boer let us build a hut and my ma picked fruit for food and clothes. After a while, she took a new man and walked on, but I stayed and worked at that place for many years. That was where I met Oupa Tok.'

'And my ma?'

'We had many children, Sienatjie – I don't remember where your ma came. They were all born in the veld. I remember there were a lot of boys and then a girl. Maybe that was your ma.'

Ouma Loos struggled to her feet, and they walked until they came to a farm gate, where Ouma Loos stopped again.

'Well, I go here,' she said.

'Do you live here, Ouma?'

'This is where I am going,' she said.

'I will come to visit you here one day, Ouma Loos.'

Ouma Loos giggled. 'Send my regards to your ma.'

'Thank you, Ouma.'

Siena hugged the old woman and kissed her cheeks.

The old lady opened the gate and, without looking back, disappeared along the track into the dark. Siena watched her go, then carried on walking towards Seekoegat. It was a relief to pick up speed and she started to run. Then the terrible thing she had done came back to her and she realised how, all that time she had been with Ouma Loos, she hadn't thought about it. Now her panic had disappeared and her mind was clear. The night was cool, and she kept up a steady trot until the veld changed with the morning sun. It was then, in the distance, she saw two small shapes, like children, walking on the road ahead.

Chapter 12

BEFORE

'It's coming, the bus is coming, it's coming.'

The boys, with aeroplane arms, were running and shouting and jumping on and off the stoep outside the classrooms. When they carried on like this, Siena went into the veld. Today, though, she ran with them to the entrance and watched the bus, a giant battered blue vehicle with 'Jesus Saves' written in white on the sides, turn off the Beaufort West road. By the time it stopped, even the screaming aeroplanes were silent behind Siena, watching and afraid. The bus hissed and shuddered as the driver switched off the engine, making Siena flinch. She had never been so close to a bus before, and she wished Hannatjie was still here to see it. Hannatjie had finished at Seekoegat Primary last year, and was back living with her father and working on the farm. It meant Siena was the most senior pupil in the school now. Almost all the others were little and, when they arrived, delivered parent-less by a welfare worker or one of the boere, she recognised the disorientation in their wide eyes and dead faces.

The driver opened his door and jumped down, almost dropping his clipboard with its white papers. Even though it was very early, his face shone in the heat.

'It's going to be hot today, hey, children?' he said. 'Are you all ready for Oudtshoorn?'

'Ja, Meneer,' they chorused, familiar with the classroom routine of answering as a group.

'And where will I find your meneer?' the driver asked.

'He is in the office, Meneer. It is this way,' Siena said, leading him to the gate and its path to Meneer Maans's office. When she could see he was heading the right way, she ran back to look at the bus.

Today, everyone was excited. All the pupils, including Siena, were wearing black shorts and red t-shirts, and Aunt Esme had tied red ribbons in the girls' hair. 'No shoes,' she'd told them. 'You understand? No shoes! I am not running around Oudtshoorn looking for your disgusting old lost shoes.' And the children had laughed and imitated her strict voice, because nobody, except Kriekie, who wore Meneer Maans's old takkies, had shoes anyway.

'Has everyone peed?' Aunt Esme was wearing a red t-shirt too, bought on the school's account, her black funeral skirt, and white takkies, which Siena had scrubbed clean for the trip. She also had with her a white hat, bought from Pep in town, and on which she had pinned a bow made from the girls' red ribbon.

'It's a long road to Oudtshoorn and there is no stopping. Have you peed? Hey?'

Everyone except for Siena, who had peed at sunrise, ran to the toilets.

'Where is Kriekie?' Aunt Esme asked her.

'He is on the bus, Aunt,' Siena said softly, hiding a smile.

'He is not allowed to do that. The bus only arrived now. Who said he could do that?'

Siena shrugged and looked at the ground.

She knew Aunt Esme was worrying that Kriekie would ruin the day. It was important to stay happy and enjoy yourself, she had told Siena last night – after all, a person didn't go to Oudtshoorn often. And, she had whispered, she had plans for fish and chips and maybe there would even be a few minutes for her to take Siena to Pep Stores to look at the clothes.

'Siena, take two boys, and fetch the lunch box and the big cooldrink bottle on the kitchen table. How did Kriekie get in this bus? The door is closed?'

The children had all watched Kriekie climb onto the roof of the bus and slide, like a snake, into an open window at the back, but now Siena pretended not to hear and walked quickly towards the kitchen to fetch the food. If Aunt Esme knew he had climbed on the roof of the bus less than one minute after it had stopped in the yard, this whole trip would be cancelled.

The bus smelt of cigarettes and disinfectant, and each window had a little curtain, tied back with a leather strap. At the very back was a small step leading to the last row, and it was here that Kriekie lay, his takkies, which had no laces but two holes where his big toes peeped through, up against the window. He ignored the children as they filed in, sitting down and then standing again to change around to be with their friends. When they saw where he was lying, they all took seats out of his reach. If the mood took him, Kriekie, even with his crippled hands, could twist a person's arm so that they would be on their knees begging for mercy.

When Kriekie heard Siena telling boys not to push and girls to settle down, he sat up. He caught her eye and, laughing, she shook her finger at him. He liked to tease Aunt Esme; this business of climbing into the bus through a window was only to get her worked up. Out of all the people at Seekoegat, he was the one who could make Siena laugh, even on those days when she walked into the veld and sat faraway from the others. He was like her – neither a farm child nor a town child, just a person from nowhere.

'At least he hasn't taken to the road,' he had once heard Meneer Maans tell the juffrou. 'That is a very positive sign for a boy like this. If he stays, then there is a chance for him … But I have seen boys like this before – they always run away.'

Kriekie watched as Aunt Esme heaved up the first step of the bus, holding on to a hand rail with one hand and summoning Siena with the other.

'O jitte, Meneer Maans should never have asked the department for this big bus. It's just too much stress for me and it's too high to get in easily.'

'Come, Aunt,' Siena said, and he watched her guide the older woman to a front seat, 'sit here, Aunt. It's very exciting to be on this big bus. Once we get going you will enjoy not having a child on top of you for the long road to Oudtshoorn.'

'O jitte, I think I must stay and you children go to Oudtshoorn.' She took a lappie from her pink plastic handbag and wiped her face. 'A person gets so hot trying to get everything done.'

When he saw Aunt Esme slump into her seat against the box of sandwiches and take her false teeth out, he knew she would soon be asleep, and he lay back and put his feet back up against the window. As soon as the old lady was snoring, Siena would come and sit by him as she had promised. The bus shuddered to life and he heard Meneer Maans, in his own car, hoot twice for it to follow him out onto the tar road and towards Meiringspoort to Oudtshoorn.

Siena loved Kriekie when he was thoughtful and quiet. He didn't resist when she took his hand, running her fingers over his palm like the juffrou had done to her that first day when she couldn't hold a pencil. Every one of his fingers was crooked, the knuckles big hard marbles.

'Why are your hands like this?' she asked.

'My fingers broke.'

'What happened?'

'I don't remember. I was small.'

'Couldn't the clinic make them straight again?'

'We never went to the clinic.'

'Look how beautiful this place is,' she said, sensing his stiffening. The bus was entering Meiringspoort, and the driver slowed to a crawl to negotiate the bends as the road criss-crossed the river that had carved the passage through the Swartberg.

'You know in all these years I have been at Seekoegat Primary School I have never been through Meiringspoort. My pa would never come here with the donkeys because he said there were too many mermaids in the river waiting to drown us and eat the donkeys. Do you think that is really true?'

'I don't know,' Kriekie said. 'Old people believe a lot of rubbish sometimes.'

Siena rested her head on his shoulder, keeping one of his knobbled hands in hers. Even though he was quiet, she knew he enjoyed her next to him. Eventually, the bus passed out of the poort and headed up the hill into De Rust.

'Maybe I better go back to Aunt Esme now. She is going to wake up,' she said.

Kriekie turned and kissed her on the lips.

'Okay, now you can go,' he said, raising his eyebrows and giving her a charming and cheeky grin.

Siena didn't know where to look. She dropped his hand and stood up. 'Okay,' she said. 'Okay, see you.' Struggling to the front of the bus, she sat down. She touched her lips and then licked them. She knew now why Kriekie hadn't taken to the road like Meneer Maans had thought he would do. It was because of her. If he hadn't wanted to stay at Seekoegat, he would have gone long ago.

They arrived at the sports field late, when the races were

already underway. There were schools from everywhere camped around the track and, when the starter gun fired, Seekoegat's pupils huddled around Aunt Esme, pulling at her new red t-shirt.

'It's the starter gun, you Karoo mamparas – who is going to want to shoot you? Hey?' Aunt Esme laughed, swatting them away. 'Come on now, show these big town school children you are not wild people from the other side of the mountain.'

Meneer Maans set up an awning at the far end of the track, and they carried the sandwich box and the big cooldrink bottle to the shade where again they huddled to watch. Each child had to run, Meneer Maans said, and he had signed everyone in for two events.

'My Seekoegat children are very fast. You can all beat these fat town children who eat KFC for supper every night.'

Kriekie was signed in to run the sprints but, when the time came for his first event, no one could find him. When the race was over he was back, sitting in the shade under the awning, sucking on one of the ice lollies the children were given on the finish line for taking part.

Siena felt surprisingly calm, even though it was the first time she had ever competed in anything. In her first race, she came second. She kept her eyes on the girl in front and was aware of the voices screaming for her to run faster. Her second event, she won, and there were wild cheers from the bottom of the field. She loved Seekoegat Primary School with all her heart, its pupils, Aunt Esme, Meneer Maans, the juffrou, and Kriekie. They were her family now; she belonged with them. They wanted her to be with them, and they wanted her to win.

One side of the track went alongside a corrugated-iron fence. It gave some shade, and children sat along it on sunburnt grass, sucking their ice lollies. At the bottom, away from the other children, where the running track turned for the home stretch, three voëltjies, not in any school clothes, sat smoking. Siena realised, as she walked back, that to get to the awning she had to walk past them, and she thought she should retrace her steps and walk the long way around to avoid getting close.

'They are rubbish boys who have no business with you. Don't look at them,' she told herself. She focused on the awning where she could see Aunt Esme handing out jam sandwiches and Meneer Maans pouring Oros into polystyrene cups.

'My girlie … Pretty girlie?' the catcalling started.

'Give me a kiss, beautiful lady …' One smacked his lips as he made kissing sounds. They all laughed but she kept her eyes on the ground.

'Don't you like me, girlie? Don't you like my beautiful body?'

'Come smoke with us, my lady. We got a nice skyfie here. Make you lekker relaxed.'

Siena couldn't help herself. 'Hou op! Shut up! You are all such rubbish, but you still think girls are interested in your ugly drug faces. Ag, puleez! Leave me alone.'

A heartbeat passed, and they were on their feet and around her. The terror of her childhood flooded back, of big boys cornering her in the lokasie when Ma and Pa were drunk and she was alone. She looked for a gap so she could escape and run.

'So you think you are fancy, hey girlie?' The voice was filled with menace, but also familiar, and her sudden panic subsided. The youth had her by the arm and was suggestively wiggling his tongue at her.

'Boetie?'

His eyes were the same – like the black pool at the bottom of the waterfall from long ago. His face was thin, his cheeks and mouth scarred. There were scabs and cuts in his hair, and she recognised ringworm.

'Is it really you? Boetie?' she said.

His smile, that was once so mischievous – and which she had looked for in the face of every boy who arrived at Seekoegat – was the same, but his little-boy lips were thin and hard.

'Siena … my jinne … Siena?'

Sensing the change in mood, and that the fun was over, the other two youths sauntered back towards the shade of the corrugated fence, looking for another girl walking alone.

'Yes, it is me, Boetie.' She took his hands. 'Sjoe, but you are so big now.' She laughed. 'You are nearly like a man.'

It had been so long since anyone had touched him and, realising how he must seem to her, Boetie pulled his hands away, but Siena, seeming to understand this and seeing the uncertainty on his face, grabbed them back.

'I am so happy to see you. For a long time I have been thinking about you,' she said. 'I thought the welfare man took you to somewhere on the N1 – I thought you were living there with your aunt and your cousins.'

Boetie looked at his feet. Her voice was so sure and she was so neat, like the larney girls who walked past the prison on their way home from the high school.

'I ran away,' he said. 'I came this side because I thought Ou Ana was in jail here.'

'But she must be out by now?'

'I never found her. They must have taken her to the jail in Cape Town and not to Oudtshoorn. I heard they took Majola there, but I have never found Ou Ana,' he said.

'Have you been back to town to look there? She could have come back.'

He should have done that, Boetie thought, but the time had passed and he had settled into a life without Ou Ana and Majola. His place, under the bush next to the prison, was still there and, when he needed to, he went there to listen to the singing and to smell the cooking coming from inside.

'Maybe Ou Ana is looking for you,' Siena said. 'How will she find you here? You should come back.'

'Where are you these days?' he asked.

'Still the same at Seekoegat Primary, but I am finishing this year and I want to go to high school. I have Sussie too. I go back to Ma and Pa on the farm in the school holidays.'

Boetie nodded. 'The same farm? With the mevrou?'

'Yes. She's there too. Still so kwaai!'

'Maybe I will come back, and then I can visit you in the school holidays on the farm.'

'I could tell you all about school,' she said.

Now Boetie kept his eyes on the ground. *I can't tell her about my life*, he thought. What was there to say? *I sniff petrol, I steal, I have killed.*

'I must go,' she said, letting his hands go. 'Come home sometime and we can find Ou Ana together.'

He nodded and looked into her eyes. 'Goodbye, Siena.' He walked back to his friends feeling stunned. As he looked back at her walking away, she looked back too, and they both laughed. Maybe it was time to go back over the mountains, he thought. He was tired of this life and he wanted to be on the farm, sitting on his koppie, watching for the dust of an approaching car and thinking about killing a porcupine for supper.

In her mind's eye, Siena saw Boetie diving under the waterfall, his laughing face with his white teeth appearing, like magic, from the black water. And then, for the first time since it had happened, she saw Ou Ana bringing the spade down on the boer's head and then him falling in the dust at her feet. The smell of his bladder letting go, the darkness and the fear came back to her. That night had been the start of it all, she thought. Once you see a person crack another's skull with a spade, smashing a tortoise is easy.

'Who was that?' Aunt Esme asked.

'Just boys watching the sport, Aunt,' she said.

'They look like voëltjies, Klimmie. Be careful, they are dangerous. You shouldn't speak to boys like that.' Aunt Esme took her arm. 'Siena?'

'It's okay, Aunt. We are going home now-now anyway.' She didn't tell Aunt Esme that the voëltjie was Boetie, and that there was no question he would be back now that he had found her again. He had given up on Ou Ana but Siena knew, after looking into his black-pool eyes, that he had never stopped thinking about her.

She wanted to go back to school now. It was hot and she was tired, so she moved into the shade away from Aunt Esme and the other children. Putting her hands under her cheek, she slept. Her dreams were filled with the curves and crevices of the mountains, and a longing for the karretjie and Pienkie and Haas.

She was asleep when Kriekie sat down against the corrugated iron with the packet of cigarettes he had taken from Aunt Esme's bag. Boetie and his friends walked over to the stranger in his school boy running clothes and, without a word, Kriekie passed up the cigarette he was smoking.

When it was time for the bus to leave for Seekoegat, Aunt Esme shook Siena awake, and she climbed on and fell asleep again in the seat behind the empty cardboard lunch box. Kriekie, who smelt of cigarette smoke, looked down at Siena as he walked past her seat, but he said nothing and went straight to the back row. This Boetie came from the other side of the mountains and, even though he was in Oudtshoorn, he knew all the places that he, Kriekie, knew. Boetie had been happy after seeing Siena again and in the mood to remember the places of his past. By the time Aunt Esme had started looking for Kriekie to tell him to get on the bus, he knew where Boetie fitted in Siena's life.

'I am in shock,' Boetie had said to him and the two others as they smoked. 'I saw this meisiekind from the farm where I grew up. She said I must visit.'

Kriekie had taken a deep drag on an Aunt-Esme cigarette and nodded. 'Ja,' he said, 'you must.'

Now, from the back window of the bus, Kriekie watched Boetie staring at them. That outjie's balance was wrong, he thought. It wasn't a good thing that Siena had told him to visit. For the rest of the bus ride home, he sat with his feet on the ground, looking at the rock walls of Meiringspoort but seeing nothing.

Chapter 13

Siena sat on the low grey-painted wall in front of the petrol station in town, waiting for the valley school bus. The oom stopped for petrol when he had money and, if he didn't, she needed to be ready to jump into the road to flag him down. The children always took the chance to buy NikNaks or Cheese Curls, but Siena had no money, only the roosterkoek with jam that Aunt Esme had packed for her and which she had eaten an hour before. In her packet, she had her comb, Vaseline, her two school books to show Ma and Pa, and her only other clothes – maroon pants and a button-up purple shirt covered in yellow daisies. She was wearing her school uniform so the old oom wouldn't give her a hard time when she took the bus; he was funny like that.

'This bus is for school children, not farm workers too lazy to walk,' he said. Not wearing school clothes meant a thirty-kilometre hike into the valley, even if you were still at school.

It had been a difficult goodbye. She had gone as far as she could at Seekoegat Primary, and now she was ready to start school in town. Thinking back, it felt unbelievable. She could read and write and do sums. And, if she wanted, she could ask the mevrou for a job in the shop on the farm. Aunt Esme said she was clever enough to work in the Spar, maybe not on a till but as a packer.

'High school!' Siena whispered it to herself. All the children she had ever known were in grade one or two, and now here she was, a girl off a karretjie, saying she was going to high school. Ma and Pa would be so proud. Meneer Maans had told her she was 'very clever' and could go all the way to matric. It was he who had signed her into the town school and, in the new year, she was going into the hostel. 'Hannatjie had the same choice, Siena,' he'd said. 'But she didn't want to carry on with school. She wanted to earn money, so I let her go. And what does she do now? Pick fruit! I tell you ... that girl chose a hard life.'

Siena remembered those conversations. She too had tried to persuade Hannatjie to carry on with school.

'Nee, Siena, I am done with books. It's too hard. I want money and 'n outjie now.'

'I am going to be a teacher one day,' Siena had said. 'I want to be like the juffrou and wear those high-heel shoes.'

'But Pep doesn't sell high heels,' Hannatjie had said. 'Where are you going to get them?'

'The juffrou doesn't buy her clothes at Pep. Those heels come from an Oudtshoorn shop.'

'So you are going to school until matric so you can buy high heels? Jy's mal. You must get 'n outjie who will buy them for you.'

But Siena wanted to go to school to learn about faraway places like Joburg and Cape Town and the sea. She wanted to understand about the people who lived there and what they ate and how they talked. Yes, a person who went to school could know those things.

When her mind came back to Ma and Pa, she thought that maybe they wouldn't be happy with her going to high school, that maybe they wanted her to pick apricots like Hannatjie. When she was leaving to come back to school after the last holiday, Ma had complained that the juffrou didn't understand Siena was needed to help with Sussie and to fetch wood. It was true, what Ma said. It was a lot for one woman to do everything and, also, if she, Siena, picked apricots, then that fifty rand every day would make Pa very happy.

'Will I be clever enough for the town school, Meneer Maans?' Siena had asked. 'There are boere children at that school and they are very clever. They will laugh when they see a karretjiemeid coming to their school.'

'Yes, there will be white children and white teachers, but forget about them. All you must worry about is your work and staying away from the boys and dop. If you do that, those white people won't say anything.' When he'd said this, Siena had looked at her feet and Meneer Maans had chuckled.

'You hear what I say now? Leave ou Kriekie here with us and we will look after him. Your worries must be about yourself now. It's arranged with the welfare man. He will organise school clothes for you, and a bed is booked in the girls' dormitory. Make sure you go to the school on 15 January, you hear? He will be there to help you. I can't be there to force you. It's up to you now.'

Siena thought about all these things as she waited for the bus. The first children from the lokasie school were wandering up the road, and she knew the bus would be along soon. Maybe she could pick apricots in the holidays and ask Pa if she could use some of the money to buy school shoes. A girl going to the town school couldn't go with bare feet. She had watched the white children getting out of cars to buy cooldrinks after school and they all wore black shoes.

The bus pulled up at the petrol pump loaded with children to be dropped off at the farms along the valley road, and Siena recognised their faces. Leroy was controlling the sliding door and she went to climb in.

'Why are you coming? Your ma and pa aren't on the farm any more,' Leroy said.

'Don't talk rubbish, Leroy, let me get in.' Siena wrestled

with him over the door and pushed it open, but she stopped when she saw all the children on the bus were quiet, watching her.

'Where have they gone?' she asked Leroy.

'Ha-ha-ha, Siena the karretjiemeid has lost her family. Maybe they ran away with some stinking donkeys and left you behind.'

The children laughed and Siena stepped back, unsure what to do. The old oom was finished at the pump and handed the petrol attendant, who had been watching Siena, a crumpled twenty-rand note.

'Leroy!' the old driver shouted. 'Los haar uit! Siena, you ma is in town now. Go look for her in the hokke. Go! I haven't got time for this today.' The sliding door slammed in her face. The oom pulled open the driver's door, arranging the cushion he kept on the front seat for his sore back, and climbed in. The engine shuddered and roared as he played with the clutch. The last Siena saw was Leroy looking back at her and laughing as the bus headed up the hill to the turn-off and was gone.

She went back to the low wall and sat down, feeling disorientated. When she saw the petrol attendant watching her, she stood and, careful not to forget her packet, crossed the veld in front of the garage and headed to the hokke. If she couldn't find Ma and Pa and Sussie, where would she sleep? The nights were dangerous in the lokasie, and she had no money and no more food. If she had to, she would go back to the garage, she thought. Maybe she could ask the petrol attendant to phone Meneer Maans. Even though there was no one at Seekoegat in the holidays, she could sleep in her own bed.

The hokke were built away from the matchbox houses. An old oom, sitting on a plastic crate in a dirt yard, pointed with his pipe to the end of the row when she asked if he knew of her parents. The last hok looked out onto the open veld and she saw that, if a person stood in the doorway, they could see the mountains without anything blocking the view. Rubbish had blown up against its corrugated-iron walls and, unlike the other hokke, there was no fence around it. Rocks held down the flat tin roof, and she saw straight away there were no windows.

Siena knocked but there was no one there. The bucket Ma used for her washing was upside down, next to the door. There was no padlock, and she untied the orange baling twine that kept it closed and pushed. The door swung open. She looked into the gloom. The small bench Pa had made many years before as a fireside seat was on one side covered with a strip of blue plastic. On it was the coffee pot, the old Hart pot that was burnt black from fire, a bowl with a spoon in it, and a mug that had lost its handle. In another corner was Pa's stool. The blanket they had used during the years on the cart was folded next to it on the dirt floor.

There was no wood or food. It was nearly supper time and Siena was hungry. At school, there would have been coffee with peanut butter bread now. She looked for a candle and matches, but there was nothing. The afternoon summer wind had come up, so she propped the door open with a rock, then spread the blanket on the ground. It was hot inside, but she lay down and, through the open door, watched the mountain slopes. Eventually, they changed from dust to pink, and then purple, and at last black.

During the night, she stirred and became aware of Ma's being there and, with her, the smell of wine. The essence of her mother – her cough and the shuffling of her feet as she took off her clothes – made Siena relax. 'Ma … Ma …' she mumbled and then, without stirring again, she let go and slept. For once, Boetie and his tortoise left her in peace but, in the morning when she opened her eyes, she felt tired and sore. Ma was next to her on the blanket and, even though the hok was stuffy, her body was pressed against Siena and her thin bare arm was across Siena's stomach, pulling her closer. She moved away from Ma, careful not to disturb her. The door was still propped open with the rock and in the grey light she could see Ma's face was thinner and her clothes were filthy. Siena could smell Ma hadn't washed, and she thought she should find water and make a fire so that when Ma woke up it would be all ready for her.

On the ground, next to Ma, was a small rolled-up orange packet of Boxer and matches. The matches were something, Siena thought – at least she could get the fire going. She collected small rocks to make a fire ring, and fed a small flame with the twigs and papers she had found in the veld. When she noticed a woman watching from the hok behind theirs, she walked over.

'Aunt, please, Aunt, I am so hungry … Please can you give me some pap.'

'I have my own mouths to feed,' the woman muttered. 'There is no money for drink in my house.'

'Aunt, I came from school yesterday and I haven't eaten. Please, Aunt, I will clean Aunt's house to pay.'

'Ag, Jirre …wait.'

The woman returned with a half-packet of mielie meal. 'There are goggas in it so you will have to pick them out when you cook. The water is over there.' She pointed to a dripping tap in the next yard.

Siena half-filled the bucket and carried it back, slopping against her legs. She set water to boil in their pot, stirring in the pap with their only spoon. When it bubbled, she pushed it onto the krummel coals to simmer. There was no salt or sugar but she knew, once she had eaten, she would feel better.

'Ma? Ma … Wake up now, Ma. Where is Pa? Where is Sussie?'

Ma sat up and, without answering her, took the bowl Siena was offering.

'Where is Pa?'

Ma made smacking noises with her lips and licked the spoon. 'When did you last eat, Ma? Where are the others?'

'There is no money.'

'What has happened to Pa's job on the farm? Why are you here alone? Where is Sussie, Ma?'

'Sussie is still on the farm with Leroy's ma … Pa is dead, Siena. Pa is dead … last month already … from the TB.'

Siena sank to her knees, pain slicing open her heart. 'My pa?'

Ma looked out the door. 'My head hurts,' she said. 'Have you got a headache powder?'

'Ma …?'

'He coughed blood and the mevrou took him to the hospital, but he didn't come back. The doctor told her the TB was in his backbone. That was why he couldn't work so lekker in the end.'

Siena remembered those times when Pa couldn't stand; when he lay curled on the ground holding his sides. 'There is a knife inside me, Siena,' he'd gasp. 'There is a knife inside, and it's twisting and stabbing all by itself.' She could see him on the karretjie, his legs spread to keep balance, the sjambok in his hand, laughing and singing, like he always did, his mouth wide open and his shoulders moving. Behind him, the veld was golden with granaatbos, and his face was turned to the sky.

What had happened to his songs, his tobacco smell, and his black-tooth smile?

'Why are you here in town, Ma?' Siena said. Her voice was

rough and she coughed. 'Why are you in this place that is not good for you? Why did you not stay on the farm?'

'The mevrou said I must go. She wanted our house for a new worker. Her men put up this hok for me.'

'Ma, the mevrou wouldn't have forced you to go. Don't lie. I know it was the dop you were chasing. Isn't it? Don't say it was the mevrou. We both know it was wine you wanted.' Ma looked away. 'Ah, Ma. You can't give up. Hope is all we have. What about Sussie? And me?' Siena shifted onto her backside, staying next to Ma, her knees bent and her head in her hands. For a while they didn't speak; the only sound was Ma scraping the bowl with the spoon. It irritated Siena, and she stood and went out, breathing in the scent of the morning veld.

'Pa,' she said, 'what will we do without you?'

The neighbour who had given her the pap came to her fence.

'Hey, meisiekind, hey, kom hierso …' The woman summoned her with a finger. 'Look here, meisiekind. It's just papsak in this hok. You need to do something.'

'Aunt, how are we going to eat?'

'Later I will take you to the pastor for some church things. Moenie worry nie. Meisiekind, you are mooi fat and strong. You must come pick apricots with me on Monday. They are big and pink and ready for picking now. We climb on the lorry at five am, there by the garage. Okay? After that, there is the onion seed – you can do that too. When you have money, you will feel better.' The woman smiled and patted her cheek.

'Please, Aunt, after the holidays I must go to school. The meneer has organised everything. Even the hostel. You see, I am going for high school.'

The woman laughed, and Siena heard in her tone mocking sympathy. 'There is no matric in these hokke, meisiekind. Here, people are hungry. If you don't come and pick, you will sit with no ma. You understand? You have a job here. You have to find a way to make a few cents to feed the two of you. Just thank God you came home before it was too late.'

In that instant, the thought of making everyone proud and going to the town school was wiped away like chalk off a board. Many times at Seekoegat, when the dream of Boetie had tormented her, she had thought about becoming a teacher and helping children write their names. There would be no more school, no sweet hostel coffee with peanut butter bread, and no school shoes.

'Meisiekind, go now and wash and tidy your hok. When I am finished with my washing, I will take you to the pastor and we can see if he will help you. Tomorrow, there is church. You must come with me so the kerksusters can see you mean business.' The woman turned away and Siena went back to the hok, but Ma was sleeping again, the pap bowl lying upside down beside her. Siena's white school shirt was crumpled and dirty from her night on the ground, and her pants had brown marks on the knees and smelt of smoke. After she'd washed and changed into her maroon pants and purple shirt, she pressed her school clothes into the bucket, wishing there was soap to scrub them. She wished she had sloppies to make her look more like an adult. Going to see a pastor without shoes didn't feel right. Before she left, she picked up Ma's bowl and spoon, and pushed them into the bucket with her school clothes too.

The aunt had said they would walk to the pastor's house at eleven. That way, if they kept him talking (or praying), he would be obliged to ask them to stay for lunch. There were a few hours to wait, and Siena walked along the gravel road until it intersected with the main road and back to the garage where she had been yesterday. It was a Saturday, and the farmers were bringing their workers in from the farms for shopping. Surely today the mevrou would come to town.

Despite the early hour, people were sitting along the grey wall. Old ladies, with wide hats and wrinkled faces, chatted as they gathered their strength to buy flour and sugar. Small children climbed around the flowerbed behind them sucking on ice lollies, their mouths stained blue. The forecourt was busy, too, as brown-legged boere in khaki and veldskoen filled their bakkies, in preparation for the long drive back to their farms.

Siena sat quietly between the people watching the vehicles. When there was a lull, the petrol attendant from yesterday walked over.

'Hullo, my suster, did you find your people?'

Siena looked up at him. 'Ja. Things are mixed up,' she said.

'I am sorry to hear that.'

'Can you phone my pa's mevrou in the valley and tell her I am back?'

The petrol attendant's attitude was gentle and he nodded. He left to help a customer, and Siena moved deeper into the shade. After a few minutes, he went into the kiosk, and when he emerged he called to her.

'Your mevrou is at the sea for the weekend. She is not coming to town today.'

'When will she be back?'

'Their picking is finished – I think she is having a nice long holiday now.'

He disappeared back into the kiosk, and a minute later came back with a white loaf, a packet of Lay's, and two litres of Coke.

'Something to make you feel better,' he said.

For the first time since she had come back to town, Siena smiled.

'Thank you.'

He smiled too. 'Have faith, my suster. Our Lord will help you.'

When Siena arrived back at the hok, Ma was gone. She laid the bread and the Lay's on Pa's bench and opened the Coke. It was cold, and she poured some in the mug and drank. Then she spread a handful of crisps on the bread to make a sandwich. The food made her head feel clearer, and she folded the blanket and hung up her wet school clothes on a bush near the hok. Then she went next door and waited for the aunt to take the rollers out her hair. The aunt said it was always important to look nice for a visit to the pastor.

'Maybe the pastor will give you a hamper,' the aunt said. 'And to say thank you to me for helping you with the pap and a picking job, I want some of it, you hear.'

'Ja, Aunt.'

'Good, but you don't say anything to the pastor, understand?'

'Ja, Aunt.'

An hour later, when they walked back to the hokke from the pastor's house, Siena was carrying a bag with two tins of pilchards, flour, yeast, beans, sugar, teabags, fish oil, and a green piece of soap. The pastor had hampers lined up against the wall in his lounge. He had asked her to tell him her story, which she did, with frequent interruptions from the aunt, who had kept saying that Ma was drinking herself to an early death. When they were finished, the pastor had taken Siena's hands and prayed.

The smell of mutton curry coming from the kitchen made the aunt's mouth water and she dabbed at her lips with a lappie taken from under her T-shirt. 'Pastor's lunch smells wonderful,' she said, widening her eyes and smiling.

'Oh, my word,' the pastor said, 'I completely forgot I have

another appointment. I must ask you if I can be excused.' He stood up and Siena stood too.

'Thank you, Pastor, for your kindness.'

The aunt heaved herself to her feet. 'Enjoy your lunch, Pastor.'

As they walked away, Siena heard the clink of a spoon on a plate and the pastor say: 'O, my jinne, but this pot smells lekker.'

The aunt rubbed her stomach, and Siena knew that she was thinking about the curry and how it tasted.

At the hok, the aunt opened the hamper and took out the pilchards and the sugar. She was about to take the soap when Siena stopped her.

'Please, Aunt, I need to wash.'

The aunt rolled her eyes and broke the soap in half.

'Monday morning,' she said. 'We walk here very early. You must be ready. This is the last time you will get help from me, so make sure you are ready.'

'Thank you, Aunt,' Siena whispered. 'Thank you for helping me.'

The aunt smiled and patted her arm. 'Dis okay, my kind. You will be just fine.'

Chapter 14

Placing a foot on the small window ledge, Kriekie used his elbows to pull himself onto the low, flat corrugated-iron roof of the room where Aunt Esme lived at Seekoegat Primary. The marks on the wall were from his previous scrabbling, an easy giveaway of his position, but the room backed onto the veld, so no one ever went around the back, and Kriekie's hiding place stayed unnoticed.

A skinny dog that Aunt Esme kept chained near the abandoned pigsty nearby gave a half-hearted bark. 'Shuddup, dog!' Kriekie said. The dog, which had the look of a German Shepherd, and which Aunt Esme kept to scare off jackals and rooikat from her chickens, was familiar with the children and, when it heard Kriekie's voice, it gave a last tired yap and lay down again.

The corrugated iron under Kriekie's feet was still warm, but it creaked as it contracted in the evening coolness. At the front corner, the branches of a pepper tree scraped against the roof in the breeze. Pink peppercorns and twigs covered the corrugated iron and the smell tickled Kriekie's nose, making him sneeze, so that the skinny dog stood again to bark. Kriekie crawled under the overhanging branches and pulled his knees to his chest. When he needed to get away from the other children, he came here.

Aunt Esme would be back from the kitchen in a while and, like always, she would guess from the way the tree moved that he was up here. And, like always, she would pretend to ignore him, carrying out her orange squash to drink while she sat on her bankie under the tree. She liked to kick off her takkies to spread her toes wide in the dusty earth. Through all this, Kriekie watched and, when she leant forwards and covered her face with her hands to pray, he too closed his eyes.

'Dankie, onse Vader, vir hier'ie kinders. Keep them safe and give me patience with them, our Father. Amen.'

When Kriekie was there, which was most nights, she added, 'Dankie, Vader, vir onse seunskind op'ie dak. Amen again!'

After a while, when only crickets and the clinking of the skinny dog's chain broke the silence of the Karoo night, she would pick up her takkies and move them inside. A person didn't want a scorpion crawling into a person's shoes, she always told the children. Kriekie thought Aunt Esme was brave that she never worried about a scorpion grabbing her big bare toes, but he knew that, if one ever did, it would be squashed and dead before it had time to raise its tail, kaalvoet or not.

When there was money for batteries and someone had been to the shops in town, Aunt Esme listened to the radio. It was always tuned to Radio Gamkaland. Mostly there were talk shows, but sometimes it was music, which was what Kriekie liked most. If he hadn't come for supper, Aunt Esme brought him a bakkie of rice and pumpkin, which she put on the bankie next to her cooldrink. The skinny dog, smelling the food, would shake his giant tick-infested ears, and Aunt Esme would get up again to throw him the old bread she had saved from the kitchen.

'Dog, I should get one of the boere to shoot you. Really, you are useless.' The skinny dog, knowing she was speaking to him, would whine and bark, and sometimes she would walk over in the dark and pat his head, telling him he was a 'mooi ding'.

The evenings were lonely at Seekoegat, but Kriekie didn't mind. He liked it when Aunt Esme pretended to tell the skinny dog her troubles. Tonight, after she had thrown the bread and patted the dog, she stood back and looked up at the roof.

'Kriekie?'

A stone landed softly at her feet.

'Your food is ice-cold. Come down and eat.'

When there was no response, she said, 'Kriekie, feeling sad for a girl you like is a normal thing. You won't be the first boy to have his heart broken. Come, stop this nonsense and get down now.'

Another stone landed at her feet and Aunt Esme, irritable now, muttered under her breath and took her cooldrink and went inside.

At night Kriekie knew Aunt Esme didn't worry about him. Since the day the welfare man had brought him, he had slept in the veld and, when he appeared at the kitchen door in the morning, even before Siena, Aunt Esme would give him his coffee and then chase him to the bathroom to wash and put on his school clothes so that Meneer Maans didn't kliek he hadn't been in the dorm. It was their secret, but Siena had known it too ... Siena, who was gone now and who wasn't coming back.

Kriekie listened to the children laughing in the dorm across the yard and then Aunt Esme moving around her room. He pulled his legs up and rested a cheek against his knees. Tears dripped onto his legs and ran down his shins, leaving wet furrows in the dust. Siena was like Dolly, he thought. She had left him and was never coming back, and now he hated them both so much, he bared his teeth and growled so that the skinny dog barked again.

'Kriekie, I am not leaving you,' Siena had said. 'I am only

going to the school in town. Don't make me feel bad now. You know I want to go for matric. With matric, I can get a sit-down job and make lekker money. You must also go for matric when you are finished at Seekoegat. The world isn't ending because I am going to school in town.'

He had looked at his hands when she'd spoken and she'd immediately taken them in hers. 'Kriekie, just because your fingers are skeef doesn't mean you can't use your head. You must read books like me. Juffrou will help you. It makes a person's brain flink.'

He thought about those times when he had waited for Dolly to come on the train with chips and green cooldrink. As if it were yesterday, that girl with blue eyes who had thrown him sweets came into his mind, and he smiled. Something happened to Dolly, he thought. So many times he had thought about walking along the railway track to Beaufort West to look for her, but he didn't know where she had gone or even whom he was looking for. Dolly had come off a farm and they had lived under the afdak. To look for a person you needed their name, and the welfare man had taken her ID. He didn't know if Dolly was her real name, or if she had a surname. He didn't know the year she had disappeared, or even if she had gone to Beaufort West like she had told him. If she was alive, it meant she hadn't wanted him. If she was dead, then she was gone, so what was the point of looking for her?

'Kriekie?' Aunt Esme must have heard him sniff. 'Please, come down now and have your food. I will sit with you while you eat. Come down now – really, your food is ice-cold.'

He stood up and climbed from the roof into the tree, and a moment later was standing in front of Aunt Esme.

'You know there is a very big boomslang living in this tree,' she said.

'Aunt, really, if there is a boomslang in this tree, Aunt would be sitting with your bankie and your cooldrink up by the tar road.'

'Don't be a Slimjan … This boomslang likes to come and go, and you sitting up there might make him decide to go, and then he is going to fall out the tree on my head.'

Kriekie laughed, and Aunt Esme leant over and rubbed his back. 'Come on now. Stop this moping for Siena. You have your own life to live. But first, tonight, ou Kriekie, I got us a Coke blikkie and I have a vleisie for you from Meneer Maans's pot.'

She opened the Coke, poured them each a glass, and for a minute neither spoke as she sipped and he ate. Eventually, Aunt Esme coughed and shifted in her seat.

'Now, tell this Aunt, how is your school work going?'

'Ag, Aunt. You know I can't do the writing.'

'Well, I must tell you, we had some news today.' Her voice took on an officious tone, and Kriekie looked at her, his brow furrowed.

'The education department is putting in a computer room here, and Meneer Maans was telling me you are number one on his list to learn how to work a computer.'

Kriekie listened, slowly chewing the meat he had dug out from under the rice and pumpkin.

'Can you think … a boy like you working on a computer? Meneer Maans says you are capable. Children these days are very clever.'

'Aunt, I can't work a computer. And you know that Meneer Maans is never going to let me touch a computer. It's very much money and I will break it. I don't want the education department's computer so that I can be in trouble when I break it.'

'O, Jirre, you are a mampara. When you leave this school, you have to do something and, with your hands, it's not going to be draadmaak or skaapskeur. You have to use your head,

Kriekie. Maybe your broken hands can be your blessing one day. It all depends on you, nè?'

Kriekie had never thought his hands were a blessing. They were claws he held to his chest to keep out the way. When children teased him, they lifted up their hands and used their elbows to nudge one another, making pik-pik-pik sounds as if they were Aunt Esme's chickens.

'Nou luister, ou seun ... these mosquitoes are biting my legs!' Aunt Esme slapped her legs, wiped a bloody mosquito onto her skirt, and continued: 'I know you are missing Siena, so come inside here by me tonight and sleep. We will pray to Jesus that Siena will get her matric and that you will learn to work a computer. You two are my big bright stars in the night sky. You must shine and make me proud.'

Kriekie smiled, and Aunt Esme leant over and pinched his cheek so that he playfully swatted her off with a crooked hand. He allowed himself to be coaxed indoors, where Aunt Esme gave him a grey school blanket. She told him to sleep under the kitchen table so that she didn't step on him if she had to go out to pee in the night. Aunt Esme's bed was at the back of the room and she relit her candle, put Kriekie's empty bakkie and their empty glasses on the table, and then sat on the bed.

Kriekie lay on his side under the kitchen table and, through the open door, watched the moon climb above the Swart-berg. Eventually, he fell asleep, thinking that Aunt Esme was a good person to be kind to him and feeling grateful for that.

Sometime in the night, he became aware of Aunt Esme's heavy snoring. He could see the outline of her body in the bed, and for a while he listened to her sighs and grunts. The blanket was rough and hot, and made him feel as if he was suffocating. He crawled out from under the table and sat on the step outside the room, studying the grey shapes of the school and the dorms where the children were sleeping.

And then, as if some primitive urge propelled him, he was up and moving like the night animals he knew so well. When he came to the barbed-wire fence that encircled the school, he held the wire up and slipped through into the veld. The skinny dog barked but, hearing nothing more, settled down. As he moved away from the school, Kriekie felt the old sense of peace he had known on those nights when he knew Dolly would soon come home. His ears and nose were as tuned into the veld as a hare. He looked back once, and then disappeared into the night.

When Aunt Esme rose in the morning, she didn't worry that Kriekie wasn't asleep under the table. Kriekie was always up at first light. Instead, she cursed him for leaving his blanket on the floor for her to bend down and pick up. Regtig, she was too old for bending down so low, and Kriekie was too big to be carrying on like a baby. He needed to learn how to sleep in a bed, wash his clothes and his body, and eat at a table with the others. Aunt Esme thought it was time she and Meneer Maans made a plan. They needed to get Kriekie right.

After she had folded the grey blanket and put it at the foot of her bed, Kriekie was the last person on her mind. She washed her face in the bucket she kept in the corner of the room, pulled on her old skirt and work blouse, and walked across the yard to the school kitchen to start the coffee and breakfast and get the children up. That night, when he wasn't on her roof, she thought it was strange that she hadn't seen him. He must be here somewhere, she thought. It was only on Monday, when Kriekie didn't come to class, that Meneer Maans phoned the welfare man.

'Kriekie has taken to the road,' Meneer Maans said.

'Well, Meneer Maans, he is not a baby. If he doesn't want to learn or stay in one place, let him go. We can't help him any more. Really, there are a lot of children who need our attention.'

'I wonder where he has gone?' Meneer Maans said.

'He will turn up,' the welfare man said. 'His type always does.'

Aunt Esme thought about Kriekie's crippled hands. She was wondering how Kriekie would eat when she brought Meneer Maans his coffee with roosterkoek and jam, and her thoughts shifted to the school's new computer centre. As he ate, and she watched him licking the jam from his fingers, she thought what a wonderful thing this was for the children of Seekoegat Primary.

It was a pity Kriekie hadn't stayed to learn computers. It might have been the one thing to help him in life.

That night, when they knew he was gone for sure, she had taken rice and pumpkin in a bakkie, just in case. When the stone didn't land at her feet, she had walked over to the skinny dog and let him gulp down the food.

'Dog, what will become of that child?' she said. 'I thought he was going to be all right.'

The skinny dog looked at her expectantly for more food, nudging her hand with his nose. 'No, Dog, there is no more. Why didn't you wake me up when he left? Hey? I really should get one of the boere to shoot you. You are totally useless.' The dog wagged its tail and strained at the end of its chain. She went back to her cottage but, instead of taking her cooldrink outside to listen for the scrabbling and sniffing of the boy on her corrugated-iron roof, she sat at the kitchen table. Outside, the old dog wached the door of the cottage, its ears cocked.

'Dear God,' Aunt Esme said out loud, 'look after your child with crippled hands.'

Then, walking over to her bed and, without taking off her takkies, she lay down and cried.

Chapter 15

NOW

By the time Siena caught up with them, the two little boys had turned in to a dry riverbed and were under a doringboom. Siena saw them sitting flat, their knees bent, in the soft dry sand. They were facing each other and, between them, digging a hole with their hands. There was a pile of twigs next to them and a small box of matches. They were very young, Siena thought, maybe about five or six.

It was only now getting light, and she had been surprised to find them, their bodies lit in gold from the early sun. After she'd reached the tar road to Beaufort West, she'd doubled back to walk along the riverbed. Seekoegat Primary was an hour's walk along the road, which ran alongside the riverbed, on high ground. There wasn't much traffic, but still the occasional bakkie made her jump. In the winters she'd spent at the school, she had grown to know this river which came from nowhere and disappeared into Meiringspoort. On freezing nights, she had listened to the burbling water and wondered where it was rushing to. Meneer Maans had said it went through the Poort, past Oudtshoorn, and all the way to the sea at Mossel Bay. Siena had never seen the sea, so she didn't know what he meant, but one day she wanted to see the place where this river finished. In the summer, when the heat dried your eyes and nose and all the children felt like splashing, the river was gone and became soft dry sand like it was now.

'This river doesn't care about the children of Seekoegat Primary,' Aunt Esme had said. 'It hides when we want to swim, but comes in a flood when we need to cross it to go to town. Really, it's a waste of a river.'

The soft cool sand was a relief for Siena's feet. She was thinking about finding a place in the shade to sleep for the day when she heard the children's voices. For a while, she sat on the far bank and watched them dig. She wanted to sit in a place where she could watch them but they wouldn't see her. They must be a labourer's children from a nearby cottage she didn't know about for them to be playing in the riverbed like this. One wore a T-shirt full of holes with dirty shorts. The other was bare-chested, his small shoulders covered in scratches from crawling under the doringbome that grew in a thicket on the riverbank. It was probably where they had been sleeping. They too were barefoot.

They look like brothers, she thought, and she wondered if she should ask them if their cottage was nearby and if she could get water and bread. Not wanting to frighten them, she crept closer, settling in the middle of the riverbed on a flat rock. If they saw her now, it would be in their own time. But they were engrossed in their digging and neither one looked up.

'The hole must be very deep, otherwise it won't cook,' said the one wearing the T-shirt.

'We must first kill it,' said the other.

'No, no, we just put it in upside down on the coals and cover it with sand. When you come back, it's dead and cooked. That's the way people do it.'

'If you eat something, you must kill it first, otherwise its spirit follows you.'

'Jissus! How are we going to kill it then?' The boy in the

T-shirt threw his hands up. 'And, there is no such thing as spirits. That's rubbish. Whoever told you that said it because you are a baby. That's just stories.' He threw a handful of sand at the scratched boy, which went in his eyes, and he started to cry.

'Eina, eina …'

'Shuddup, you big baby.'

The boy with the scratched back stumbled towards a bottle of water propped against a rock, and poured a little in his hands to wash his eyes. The other boy watched him and then went back to his digging. The scratched boy was quiet for a long time, and Siena smiled as she watched him. It was sweet, that – thinking that if you didn't slaughter something properly, its spirit would follow you. Pa had told her that too when she was small, when they were still on the karretjie. Maybe these were karretjiemense.

'With a rock,' the scratched boy said, 'we must klap it with a rock.'

They were like two old men arguing over how to make potjiekos, and she wondered what it was they were going to catch and cook. The way they had prepared the hole for cooking was like the karretjiemense. Pa had done that too. It was a veld-oven, a way of cooking that had been passed on from one to the next since humans had found fire. Siena looked around to see if there were donkey cart tracks or droppings, but there was nothing.

The one in the T-shirt sighed. 'It's deep enough – let's make the fire.' He stood, picked up the matches, and walked to the riverbank to pull up a tuft of brown grass as a fire lighter.

'Hold this,' he said to the other boy.

In the morning quiet, the burning grass crackled and the flames leapt. The scratched boy had moved the twigs into the hole, and he dropped the burning grass on top of them so that soon there was a roaring blaze with grey smoke wafting down the riverbed to Siena.

It was then, as the boys turned to find more sticks for their fire, that they noticed her. The one in the T-shirt walked over and was about to speak when he saw the blood on her clothes.

His black eyes changed, and she saw he was wary.

'Did you slaughter something?' he asked. 'Aunt must get other clothes.'

'I want to sleep,' she said.

'You have got blood on you. You smell like blood.'

Pointing to a patch of shade, she said: 'If I sleep there, promise me you won't bother me.'

The boy frowned. 'We have made a fire to cook,' he said. 'We are very hungry.'

'Yes, what will you eat?'

The scratched boy had disappeared, but was now struggling down the bank, carrying what looked like a rock in his arms.

'I have got one!' he shouted. 'I've got one!'

The boy in the T-shirt ran back to him and Siena stood. When she saw it was a big old tortoise, that they were turning upside down to bury in the burning hole, she screamed. Her voice rang in her ears and echoed along the riverbed, sending Namaqua doves and sparrows into the golden blue. A Karoo hare shifted in the brush, its heart pounding, and a bat-eared fox pricked up its giant ears and stood, ready to run. The small scratched boy dropped the tortoise, bolting back up the bank from where he had just come.

'You can't do that! You can't kill a tortoise.' Her voice was hoarse from screaming.

The tortoise landed on its feet and moved off down the riverbed. Its tough grey legs stretched out to give it speed, its ancient clawed toes leaving half-moon tracks in the sand. The boy in the T-shirt watched it and then, ignoring Siena, added more twigs to the smouldering fire.

'That is an old man of the Karoo. He is the only one who was here at the time of our ancestors. Why have your mothers not told you about the tortoise? What is the matter with the two of you?'

The boy in the T-shirt turned to face her, his black eyes hard, his face unforgiving. There was a flicker of familiarity in his expression, and Siena thought she had seen him before. 'We can't worry about ancestors when we are so hungry,' he said.

'Why are you so hungry? Go back to your karretjie and tell your pa to stop with his trek here and trek there. He must get a farm job so he can feed you. You must eat pap and sugar, not tortoises.'

'Aunt,' the boy paused and looked into her eyes, 'we are not hungry from yesterday but from before yesterday and before that too. If we can't eat an old man tortoise, then we will die. And, where must we get pap and sugar anyways?' And then, as if to calm her, he said: 'We will give Aunt some of the meat. I think Aunt is also very hungry.'

'Where is your karretjie? Where is your mamma?'

'Mamma ...?' The boy in the T-shirt frowned and turned away.

'Seuntjie, are your people near here? Where is your karretjie?'

Sensing Siena had calmed down, the scratched boy crawled out of his hiding place and cautiously walked across the sand towards her. When he saw the dried blood on her clothes, he reached out and touched it, not with a finger, but with his knuckles. Siena wanted to ask him why he touched her like that, but, when he looked up at her, there was such pain in his eyes that instead she put her hands on each side of his face.

'Who are you?' But still he didn't speak. 'What are you boys doing here alone? Where are your people?' He started to cry then, and Siena sat in the sand, pulling him down with her. 'It's okay, ssshh, ssshh, I will help you.'

The boy in the t-shirt came over then too and sat next to her, resting his head on her shoulder. 'I am sorry I screamed and shouted,' she said. 'But, really, tell me now, where are your people?' The boy in her arms sighed deeply; still, neither child responded.

It was hot, and Siena moved them all into the shade. The fire had gone out and the tortoise had disappeared. Under the tree, the scratched boy slept in her arms. The other one curled up next to her, his ribs rising and falling as he slept, his head on her thigh. Later, the three of them could walk to Seekoe-gat Primary, she thought. Aunt Esme would feed them. She closed her eyes and dozed, thinking of school, and that these boys should go to Seekoegat and learn to make their s's and h's. When they were awake, she must ask their names to hear what letters they would need to learn first. The juffrou always made the new children start with their names.

In the afternoon, when the sun was dropping behind the mountains and the shadow of the doringbome stretched al-most all the way across the sand, Siena awoke. She thought she heard someone calling her name, and she felt disoriented from sleep and lack of water and food. The boys were gone. She looked up and down the riverbed to see where they were playing, but there was no sign of them.

'Siiieeennnnaaa … Siiieeennnaaa …' She stood and stum-bled. When she found her balance, she moved towards the voice but fell again, and for a while she stayed on all fours before she lay on her stomach. Her throat was dry, her voice hoarse, so that when she tried to call back nothing came out.

It was like this that Meneer Maans found her.

She was lying in the sand, her eyes closed and her knees

pulled up. He shook her shoulders to rouse her, but she didn't respond.

'Esme, she's dead. We have come too late.'

Aunt Esme was barefoot, her sandals in her hand, and breathless from exertion.

'Klimmie? Klimmie? Is ekke, dis Aunt Esme.'

She touched Siena's lips, running a finger over the cracks and blood.

'Nee, nee, she is breathing. Meneer, she is alive. Dear God.' She forced open one of Siena's eyes, leaning in close to study the sunken, dehydrated eyeball.

'O Hemel, we must get her to the car ... O, Liewe Jesus, my arme kind. Meneer, help me. Come, we must lift her.'

Siena, aware of being picked up off the sand, smiled.

Aunt Esme. Meneer Maans. She was at Seekoegat Primary. She had made it.

In her mind, she told them about the two brothers – how she had found them making a fire in the riverbed to cook a tough old tortoise. She laughed when she thought about it. They must come to the school. There was coffee and bread for all of them there. Ja, Meneer Maans could be kwaai but it was a wonderful place really, and when she looked back on her life, the time at the school was the happiest she had ever been.

They lifted her to her feet and, with her arms slung across their shoulders, they walked her to Meneer Maans's car, which was parked a short way from the tar road. He held a bottle of water to her lips, saying they should go straight to town and the hospital, but Siena shook her head. 'Nee, nee ...'

When she had drunk water and her rasping dry voice had returned, she said she couldn't leave the two starving boys who were trying to find food in the dry riverbed.

'They are very small, Aunt Esme. These are children who need to be looked after. They are from a karretjie,' she said.

'They were going to eat a tortoise … A person should never eat a tortoise.'

She was on the back seat, and she lay down and closed her eyes again.

'Esme, wait here, I will see if I can find these children and tell them to come back with us in the car,' she heard Meneer Maans say. 'Give her as much water as she can take.'

'Where are they?' Aunt Esme asked when he returned to the car.

He shook his head. 'There is nothing there, Esme, not even a child's footprint,' he whispered.

'But she said they dug a hole and made a fire, and that she stopped them from cooking a tortoise … There must be the hole and the coals from the fire?'

Meneer Maans looked at Siena lying across the back seat and shook his head.

'Daar's niks,' he said under his breath.

Aunt Esme's eyes widened and she nodded. 'Let's get her back to the school,' she said. 'She must drink salt water now and then her mind will come right.'

At the school, Aunt Esme led Siena to the girls' bathroom and held her up as the water streamed over her bloodied body. Then she scrubbed her with one of the children's lappies and Lux. The feel of the water and the smell of the soap brought Siena to life and the old woman was able to let her go so she could wash herself. When she was dry, Siena dressed in a skirt and T-shirt from the donation box. At the table in the kitchen, she took in a little of the salt water, and then asked for sweet coffee and bread.

'That's my girl,' Aunt Esme said. 'You are fine now.'

While Siena was eating, Aunt Esme pushed the blood-covered maroon pants and the purple shirt with its little yellow flowers into the old wood stove, where the coals glowed red and the clothes shrivelled and took flame until there was nothing left.

'Aunt Esme, how did you know where to find me?' Siena asked.

Aunt Esme smiled. 'Tonight, Klimmie, you must rest, and when you wake up, everything will be clearer.'

'Has Meneer Maans called the police?'

'You relax now. There are no police.'

When Siena finished eating, Aunt Esme lit a candle and they crossed the dusty playground in the dark. The old lady helped Siena onto her bed and lay down next to her. Outside, the skinny dog barked and then whined at something moving in the veld. Aunt Esme blew out the candle, covered her face in her hands, and said her nightly prayer.

'Dear God, thank you for bringing our Klimmie back to us. Thank you for my children. Amen.'

Chapter 16

BEFORE

Boetie stretched his legs, shifting so the curve of the rock fitted into his back. His fingers were knitted over his brow to shade his eyes as he watched the comings and goings in the valley. During the night, his bare feet had found the old path over the shale between clumps of hard grass and Karoo bush up the koppie. It was the same, as if no one had been to the top since he was last here all those years ago. His sitting place … what he could see … knowing where people were … even the wind – it was all familiar, and for once he was at peace. The longing inside him – that feeling that had chewed at him like a rat when he was in Oudtshoorn – was for this place and his people who were gone now.

Smoke from Leroy's mother's lunch fire drifted up the slope, and the doringhout smell made him a boy again, watching for Baas Jan's bakkie and thinking that, if the boer brought flour and yeast, Ou Ana could make roosterkoek. In a lucerne field below, the oubaas was driving a tractor. Its droning made him drowsy, and he closed his eyes. Workers called to one another and he could hear laughing. A lamb bleated and, on the ridge, as always, the baboons barked. He opened his eyes to watch them climbing the rock face like daredevils, while the old troop leader sat apart, looking down on the valley and probably him. The hok where he had lived with Ou Ana and Majola was under the ridge. He held up a finger, like he had done when he was little, and, keeping its tip steady on an outcrop, moved his eyes down to the hok directly below. What would have happened if the baboons had pushed a rock down? Ou Ana or Majola could have been killed. He wondered if a person could hear a rock falling, or if it landed on you and you were dead. He imagined Ou Ana there, sitting on her plastic crate, elbows on her knees, blue tobacco smoke curling around her head; Majola wasn't far off and, in his mind, Boetie heard the thud of an axe as he chopped wood. It was just as well baboons were animals and didn't push rocks off cliffs onto people below.

He had been surprised the hok was in one piece, hidden by thorn trees that no one had cut back. He thought the valley workers would have taken the corrugated iron for their chicken coops and pig pens, but they had left it untouched. It was because of the murder – he understood that. To take from killers was to brush against the devil, and so they stayed away, not wanting to go near the place where Baas Jan's vengeance-seeking ghost with its fire eyes walked with a shotgun. Yet their children had been inside. There were the remnants of games scattered on the dirt floor, and they had broken off the wooden door Majola had once struggled to hang. The nail Majola had hammered through the corrugated iron to hang his jacket was there and, in the bush at the back, Boetie found Ou Ana's shoe crusted with dried mud and perished from the sun. She had gone to jail with one bare foot, he thought. There had been no chance for her to find her other shoe. Majola and Ou Ana had not come back here. If they were finished with jail, they would have crept along the valley road in the dark and come home, even to nothing.

Baas Jan's farm was the same, and Boetie thought the dead man's family was waiting for his blond red-faced son to grow up and take over. He would come eventually, like his father, in an old bakkie with a beaten-down woman beside him, starved workers on the back, and a shotgun wedged between the seats. The workers would break apart the hok and turn its corrugated-iron walls into a new shack under a different thorn tree. Maybe the red-faced son would keep pigs in the cement dam, and a boy would have to find watermelons to feed them so they wouldn't die of hunger and thirst. Maybe too these workers would wait for the bakkie to come so they could be paid with weevil-flour from the oupa's shop. Baas Jan's furniture was still in the house, broken and upturned by the baboons that had come in through smashed windows. Boetie had climbed in to look around the place. A stiff and dirty sheepskin, which he had once seen through the kitchen window on a chair, was on the floor. He picked it up and righted a chair, and put it back where it had been against a wall. He sat in the chair for a long time during his first night back, enjoying the softness of the wool, and imagining there was a brandy and Coke on the table in front of him. The rough painted walls were stained by bat droppings, and the baboons had messed everywhere, even on the mattress, which had been stripped. Outside, the plough, hidden by weeds, was pushed up under a tree where Majola had left it, and the black coals from Baas Jan's braai fire so many years ago remained trapped in a stone circle near the backdoor.

Boetie had come back three nights ago, cutting through the veld, away from the road with its workers' cottages and barking dogs. The river was flowing and he'd waded in, feeling his way over its slippery bed with his bare feet. The water meant he had not needed to go near people straight away, although he knew he would soon need to ask for food. He had gone to the hok first, circling it in the moonlight and running his fingers over its rusted corrugations. Ou Ana's crate had been pushed in a corner, and he'd put it back under her tree, sitting on it under the stars and smoking. Later, he had walked into the bush and found the spot that someone had marked with two planks and a nail where they had buried Baas Jan that night after Ou Ana had hit him over the head, and which the police had discovered so easily. What no one had found was the spade that Ou Ana had used and which Boetie had propped against a tree deep in the bush, as if a worker had forgotten it. The spade was still there, against the same tree, as he had left it.

He wanted to ask people in the valley about Ou Ana and Majola and where they were. The mevrou would know, but he couldn't bear her ice-blue eyes with their gaan-gaan look. She would see the hard times in his face and later, when she was drinking tea, she would tell the oubaas that Boetie was back, and that his dead look and scarred face made her skin crawl. He had never been her child with a birthday cake and school uniform. Baas Jan was the one who should have seen to his schooling, who could have spoilt him a little, but Boetie knew that Baas Jan had cared about nothing except his brandy and his shotgun.

'Hy kan 'n witman wees, maar hy bly gemors,' Majola had said. Yes, Baas Jan had been white, but even Majola, who didn't matter to anyone and was in jail in Cape Town for murder, knew he was rubbish. Majola was nobody, but he had been more than Baas Jan. It was because that gemors was dead that he, Boetie, had been pushed to the outside. When he showed his face at the farmhouse door, the oubaas would tell the mevrou to telephone the police to pick him up. They didn't need trouble again.

On the long walk into the valley, Boetie had thought he should ask the mevrou for a job. He could lower his eyes and make an excuse for himself, telling her, 'Ek kry swaar,' and maybe she would say he could pick fruit or work sheep. If he lived quietly with his mouth shut and his eyes down, he could become one of them and one day marry a girl from the valley, and their children would be given cake and school clothes. But he knew the valley people would hold in their hearts the feeling that he was an inkomer from no-good blood and, while he would sit by their fires, they would never laugh in the same way with him as they did with one another. They would remember that Baas Jan had found Majola and Ou Ana and a small boy on the vlaktes, and he'd brought them into the valley on his bakkie.

Boetie tried to remember what had been before Baas Jan, but all that came to him was the wine smell and arms that held him too tight. In Oudtshoorn, no one had cared where he was from or what his story was, but that place was big enough for people not to care. What mattered there was his blade and the rage inside him.

He had come to find his people, but he would not stay in the valley now. The mountains leant in too close so that he wanted to shout and kick. Maybe that was why Ou Ana and Majola weren't here. If they were free, they could have gone on to the vlaktes to look for work, or maybe they were in town. Maybe they felt like he did; maybe they needed to see the horizon so they could breathe.

On the road below the koppie, Leroy, in blue worker's overalls, was walking home for lunch. He was short, but his shoulders were thick and he strutted like a kapok. Boetie thought Leroy was the kind of man who organised prayer meetings, spoke at funerals, and was always sorting out souls weaker than himself.

Ja, Leroy, gaan huis toe.

Go sit like a little rooster and eat the food your mother has spread out for you. Ja, thank God for your blessings. Eat meat and rice and drink coffee. Have a lie-down before your mother wakes you up to go back to work.

'Kom, Seun, opstaan; the oubaas has things for you to do.'

'Ag, Ma, die lewe is maar swaar. Ai, but a man must work.'

Did you sleep well, Leroy? Today I am not in the mood for fighting. And I will leave your old mother, who spends the day alone in the yard, clucking to her chickens. You can have your life of labour, bowing to the oubaas, Leroy. I don't care enough to take you from it. It was luck for you, Leroy. You could have been me, sitting on the koppie, feeling your stomach twisting for bread and staring at your bare feet.

Boetie shook his head. Even if he had Ou Ana and Majola and a farm job, he wouldn't have been like Leroy, handing his pay packet to his mother on a Friday and waiting for church on Sunday. If he had been born into a valley family, he would have been the boss in his house. And he wouldn't have wasted time with a church pastor telling him what to do all the time. Maybe, if he had been born into a different life, he would have been like Ou Ana and been sent to jail for smacking the baas on the head with a spade.

The afternoon wore on and he dozed, moving onto his side, with his head in the shade of a rock. He dreamt he was fighting the boy near the garage in Oudtshoorn again and, as they fought, the boy cried out, 'Mamma … Mamma …' Boetie wrestled with him and, in his dream, there was the glint of a street light on a knife. Over and over, he stabbed and, when at last the boy was dead and the crying stopped, it was a relief. He awoke sweating and thirsty, with his fists clenched and a blood taste. His body was stiff and he sat up, rubbing his face and licking his lips. The baboons were gone, and the oubaas was driving the tractor back to its afdak. Boetie's head throbbed. He sucked in a deep breath, but when he exhaled, it caught in his chest and there was no air. The thundering in his head was in his heart too, as his chest squeezed. He fought for an even rhythm, in-and-out, panting like a dog. Still, there was no air. What came was a gurgle that made the muisvoëls in a tree on the road flutter. He fell onto his side, knees pulled into his chest, as the sobbing convulsion grabbed at his shoulders and shook him like a violent man.

When night came, Boetie made his way down the koppie to Leroy's mother's house, stumbling and sliding on the shale. There were men around the fire; he knew that what was making them laugh would fade when they saw him. The dog barked and Leroy, who sat facing the path into the yard, rose, handing his coffee mug to one neighbour and his cigarette to the other.

'Ja? Wies'it?'

When the dark shape stumbled, Leroy moved around the fire. At the same time, Boetie reached the corner of the cottage and the circle of light, steadying himself against the wall.

'My jitte! Are my eyes telling me the truth?' Leroy said.

Boetie lurched towards him, and the men, with their coffee and cigarettes, stood as one as Leroy put out his arms, catching him as his legs caved.

'Joh! You look like a man who needs coffee and food. Ma? Ma? Bring something for this man, Ma!'

The old lady appeared in the doorway. 'En nou?'

Boetie turned towards her voice.

'Ma, it's Boetie. Ou Ana and Majola's boy. Remember, Ma? Bring him coffee, Ma.'

'Wat soek hy hier?'

'Ma!'

The circle around the fire opened and Leroy helped Boetie to a plastic chair.

'Jinne, maat, jy lyk sleg!'

The old lady shuffled from the doorway with a mug, muttering and watching. Boetie reached for the coffee and, for an instant, Leroy held on to it too when he saw Boetie's hands were unsteady.

'Bring him bread, Ma.'

The bread came and Boetie dipped it in the sweet coffee. When he finished, someone passed over a cigarette, and all the while the men whispered and waited.

Leroy sent his mother for a blanket and then handed it to Boetie. 'This is a good fire. Sleep here, and I will build it up for you.'

Boetie nodded.

'Reg, manne,' Leroy said, 'I am going to call it a night. There is work to be done in the morning.' They went unspeaking into the dark, unsure and uneasy.

Leroy returned to his chair, lit a fresh cigarette and passed it to Boetie.

'Brother, what are you doing here?'

Boetie looked into the flames, feeling the heat of his face, and sucked hard on the cigarette before handing it back.

'I came to find them.'

'Ja, we thought you would. We thought you would come back long ago.'

'Do you know where they are?'

'They never came here. Nothing has happened on that farm since … since Baas Jan was murdered.'

Boetie nodded.

'That girl, daai karretjiemeid, the one whose people took you in, Siena, she's back.'

Boetie looked up. 'Here?'

'No, in town.'

Boetie put his mug down.

'Why don't you sleep now, my brother, and in the morning,

I will give you clothes and shoes and you can wash. Then you can make a start.'

Siena …

'Leroy?'

'Yes, my brother?'

'Where in town is she?'

'She works at the garage. When her pa died, we helped the ma with a hok. It's there, on the edge of the lokasie. I think she will be happy to see you, to have a man in the house.'

Boetie lay down by the fire, pulling the blanket over him.

'I will go tomorrow,' he said.

Leroy smiled. 'That's a good plan, Brother,' he said. 'Your people are not in the valley any more. There is nothing for you here.'

Chapter 17

The night closed around Siena as she headed towards the lo-kasie and away from the fluorescent brightness of the garage forecourt. It had been a twelve-hour shift, and her hands were chapped and stank of petrol. Fridays were always busy. Wages were paid and there were long queues at the pumps while those on foot jostled for bread and tobacco. The walk to the hok was quickest through the veld, and it was the way she came when one of the others was with her. Tonight, she was alone, so she took the long way home. The footpath over the rise between the main road and the lokasie was deserted, and she ran until she was under the street lights and between the houses again. The houses were simple buildings inhabited by people born into poverty but reaching towards middle-class. Old Toyotas stood under afdaks, and through windows she saw children with bowls of rice and mutton stew on their knees watching TV. Yes, Siena thought, tonight was a night for stew. Sussie would have put on the pot with the braaisak she had sent home. The thought of the stew-pot made her walk a little faster.

The lights in the pastor's house were on and cars were parked in the street. On Fridays, the elders and their wives held a prayer meeting and afterwards a bring-and-share. The brother from the garage would be there once he'd finished on the computer. It was why he was desperate for them to balance the till tonight – so he could eat braaied chops with cabbage and carrot salad, made with condensed milk and mayonnaise, and drink green cooldrink. She smiled at the thought of him, and how he loved the elders' prayer meeting.

'Oh, Siena, we have very important talks with the pastor,' he'd said. 'Our people are losing their lives to the devil's evils of drink and drugs.' To impress her, he had added: 'And in the summer, we take our "bring" out to share by the pool.'

That pool.

Now that made Siena smile. She had seen it just that once, through the pastor's lounge window, when the aunty had taken her to ask for a food hamper. She hadn't known what the pool was for until many months later, when she was work-ing at the garage, and the brother had talked about sitting be-side the pool, that she'd realised that was what she had seen. That the pastor had been able to carve such a deep hole out of the dry Karoo earth amazed her. Surely only God could make such a big hole in such hard ground? A mermaid would like to live in a pool like that, waiting to grab a person's ankles to pull them under. For sure, Boetie wouldn't have been afraid to swim in that pool. No, he had loved the black depths under the waterfall, so he wouldn't have worried about a blue pool in a pastor's yard. But, in all the time she had known about the pastor's pool, she had never heard of it having water in it. Maybe there wasn't enough water in the Karoo to fill a big hole like that, she thought. Maybe, if the pastor filled it, there would be nothing left for the people to drink.

The evening was cool and, when she passed the new match-box houses, doors that always hung open were shut. In some yards, fires burnt in drums and the shadows of men crouched low around them. She glanced behind her, feeling that some-how tonight was different, but there was no one there.

After that day, when she'd come back from Seekoegat Primary and found Ma and the hok, and learnt that Pa was dead, Siena had expected nothing more. When she thought about it now, the idea of going for matric had been a crazy one. If Pa had been alive, he would have told her they needed her to work, and Ma would have moaned and complained that she needed Siena to help with Sussie. Now, thank God, they had the hok and it was home. Without her wages, they would starve. She never allowed herself to think about going for matric or what might have been. Tonight, as she walked through the deserted streets, she wondered if they could qualify for a government matchbox house. A matchbox had windows, an inside toilet, a tap, and a door that locked. The hok cooked like an oven in summer and, in the winter, they coughed and sneezed as the dry cold blew through the corrugated-iron walls. Still, she was grateful; people had been kind, and life wasn't bad. The brother had helped her with a cleaning job at the garage shop all that time ago, after her first and only apricot season had finished. When, at last, she had become a petrol attendant, there had been enough money to buy Sussie's clothes and flour for bread. The brother had taught her to do the computer work and, truly, she had found it very easy, even though the brother complained all the time that it was difficult. Last week, the women in the hokke, always bent over their buckets doing washing, had straightened up to watch the Lewis Stores flatbed bump along the track to Siena's place. Even the aunty next door had come to watch as a new table and four chairs were off-loaded. Sussie had danced around the hok and tried every chair so that Siena and Ma had laughed until their faces hurt. Next, Siena had told them, she was planning to buy a cupboard for their special things. There was one, cream with gold handles, at Lewis that she liked. She'd pulled Sussie into her arms and, as the child looked up, Siena had whispered to her: 'And after the cupboard, I am going to buy us a TV.'

They were happy. And even though Ma drank, they didn't fight.

Their yard was fenced to keep out dogs, and to stop people taking a shortcut into the veld and tramping on their garden. Siena and Sussie had planted geranium cuttings, like she had seen Aunt Esme do at Seekoegat Primary, and a patch of grass at the front where they could sit on a nice day. With a borrowed pick, Siena had hacked out a hole in the shale and lined it with manure for a small tree. 'If we look after it, then its roots will find a way through the rock to the underground water and it will grow big, and one day we will have nice shade,' she'd told Sussie. Even Ma loved the tree, tipping her dirty washing water at its base. With river stones, they paved a pathway to the hok's entrance and planted spekboom along each side to make the place greener. Around the back, Siena had the aunt's no-good son put in poles and string wire for their washing line. Ja, she thought, it had been a hok slammed together by people who hadn't wanted them, but now it was their home.

In the picking season, the aunt still went on the trucks, but more often than not she was at home. As Siena passed her hok now, she heard the familiar tone of her bossy voice as she fought with her son. It was always the same fight. He ate heartily from his mother's pot but smoked dagga while she was picking.

'You must look for work!' she shouted.

'There is nothing, Ma.'

'Go to the farms, then.'

'Can you not understand? There is nothing, Ma.'

When there was no picking work, the aunt asked in town for domestic jobs, but it was Siena who bought the flour for the aunt's bread. Sometimes, on the way back from the garage, she stopped and invited the aunt to come for sweet tea. Tonight, she hesitated; the aunt was in the fighting mood and the air didn't feel right. Maybe next time … Besides, she needed to get home to check on Sussie.

Siena smelt cigarette smoke, not the syrupy tang of Boxer rolled in newspaper that Pa had smoked and which Ma preferred, but a real cigarette. As she opened the gate, she saw the smoker in the yard, standing at the side of the hok, in the deep shadow where she couldn't make out his face. The red tip of his cigarette moved from his side to his mouth and then down again as he exhaled.

'Yes, can I help you?' she called as cold fear swirled around her like the dust devils that raced around the veld. 'Who is there?'

The smoker dropped the cigarette. The grinding of his shoe on the shale as he put it out made the world slow down so that she heard nothing else. If she screamed, the aunt and her no-good son might hear. Siena could use a smooth river stone from the garden to hit him. He stepped from the shadow into the dull light from the moon and the distant street light and, in an instant, the shape of his nose, the set of his eyes, and his half-smile came back to her.

'Boetie?'

'Hullo, Siena.'

'O jinne, Boetie. This is such a big surprise. Joh! Now you are really the last one I was expecting to see. Ek het nou lekker geskrik. You nearly made me scream. Why didn't you wait where I could see you? I thought you were a skollie waiting to rape me.'

'Nee, Siena.' He laughed.

She took his hands and pulled him close, but the hug was stiff and unfamiliar.

'Do you know, I was thinking about you right now as I was walking and, *pooofff*, here you are! I wondered after that time, when I saw you at the school sports in Oudtshoorn, if you would ever come back.'

'Ja. I wanted to find Ou Ana and Majola, but they are gone. Nobody here even remembers who they are.'

'Maybe they are working on one of the farms along the N1. Town people don't always know everybody.'

He followed her to the door, and for a second she felt unsure about what he wanted.

'Have you not seen Ma? She is always here with Sussie?' she asked, as if he remembered her people, but then she thought it was only Ma whom he would know. The door was unlocked, as it always was for Siena when she was expected from work, and a candle flickered on the table. Sussie was asleep on her mattress, her grey blanket pulled over her head, but there was no sign of Ma. Siena lit the paraffin lamp so she could see Boetie properly. He was good-looking, she thought, but something in his eyes – once so keen and full of life – had changed, and she sucked in a breath.

'How long have you been back?' she asked.

'I came last week,' he said. 'I heard you were at the garage.'

'Regtig? You knew and you didn't come say hullo? You are a real bliksem.' She swatted him playfully and he smiled again. 'Come, there is lekker food in the pot. Sit down and let me warm it for us.'

Sussie stirred, and Siena watched as he glanced at the child and then at the other mattresses, each one made with a pillow and a blanket folded at the foot.

'Are you looking for work?' she asked.

'Miskien.'

Siena dished up the stew, giving Boetie the bigger portion and, before she sat to eat, she set the kettle to boil.

They ate in silence. Siena saw he was hungry, but she made no more comment. When she was finished, she scraped her bones into the bin and poured boiling water on teabags and sugar in two mugs. When they were done, he made no move to go.

'I must sleep now, Boetie. The shifts at the garage are very long and I am working tomorrow.'

He stood up and walked to her mattress.

'I need to stay here,' he said, 'until I am settled.'

'Oh. Okay. That is my place.'

He took his shoes off and lay down on her pink pillow, covering himself with the grey blanket. Siena poured water from their bucket into a plastic bowl to wash their plates and the pot. In the dull light, she studied his back. He had nothing with him; he had the smell of someone who hadn't washed for a long time. When she was finished, she took the dish water to pour out at the base of the little tree and, like she always did, she left the yard and walked a little way into the veld to sit on the big rock and think.

'He always was a no-good rubbish.'

'Pa?'

'We should never have encouraged him. Everything you have made here for Ma and Sussie he will destroy. He can't help himself.'

'No, Pa, he is just a person who had no choices.'

'Prr!'

'Well then you tell me what I must do, Pa, because I can't chase him away. Look at him – he has nothing.'

'Get rid of him, Siena. Find a way.'

Siena saw the shape of Ma coming down the road, and she ran to meet her and keep her quiet. When they were in the hok, she helped Ma onto the sponge and lay next to her.

'What is going on in this hok?' the aunt next door demanded to know when Siena filled her bucket the following morning.

'Aunt, it is just my brother who has come back from Oudtshoorn,' Siena said politely. 'He needs a place to stay until he finds a job.'

'Job se gat! That's not a brother – that's a skelm! And where did you come with a brother out of nowhere? Hey? Look in his eyes, Siena. There is something else going on there. I like nothing of this! We don't want his type here. He must voetsak …'

'No, Aunt, he needs a place for a while. We must help him. It won't be for long.'

'That one has a tik face, Siena. If he is in your hok, then Sussie must come to me while you are at work. I am telling you, I like none of this.'

Chapter 18

There were two things Kriekie wanted to do in town. He could have avoided the trip by giving one of the others fifty rand to buy him dagga. This was what he always did when word came that the farmer was going on Saturday morning and there was space on the bakkie. But, this time, Kriekie wanted to go himself because he wanted to buy dagga and he wanted to find Siena. And, if he did, he wasn't coming back.

'What are you looking for in the town?' one of the others said when he saw Kriekie squatting next to the bakkie.

Kriekie ignored him and moved off to wait in the shade.

'Maybe hy't 'n girlfriend,' said another, and the farm workers waiting for the farmer laughed.

'Nee, he is too ugly for a girlfriend.'

'Maybe he is going to buy a TV.' They all laughed again. Kriekie stayed on his haunches. He knocked the ash from his pipe and pressed in fresh tobacco, prodding it with a match, before he lit it and took a deep drag. The farmworkers lost interest when he didn't react, rolling cigarettes and lighting pipes as they waited. There was excitement in the smoke-smelling morning air; there always was when they were going to town.

The farmer stepped out the kitchen door, his hair combed back with Brylcreem, khaki socks pulled to his knees and his old brown leather briefcase with all his papers under his arm.

The workers rose and greeted in unison. 'Môre, Meneer…'

'Môre,' he said without breaking stride.

Two by two, they climbed onto the bakkie, the women pulling one another up, the men passing up babies. As he reached the bakkie, the old Afrikaner noticed Kriekie squatting under the tree and paused. He said nothing, but Kriekie could see his thought process as he tossed his briefcase onto the passenger seat, climbed in, and started the engine. It was the first time Kriekie had ever waited to join the crowd going to town and, like the farmworkers, the boer was thrown off balance. Kriekie was the last on and struggled to close the tailgate, until one of the others jumped down and, with deft hands, pushed down the giant clasps. Always there was a hubbub on the bakkie on a Saturday morning and, even with Kriekie there, the farmworkers talked and laughed and teased.

Kriekie stood on the bakkie, holding on to the tralies as best he could so that he didn't fall as the vehicle bumped along the eight-kilometre track. At last, it crossed the cattle grid that led onto the smoothness of the tar road. There was nowhere on this farm he didn't know, but he felt no nostalgia about leaving. This was his Karoo and, wherever he went, he would find the burrows and bossies, koppies and klippies that made it home. He knew they were all startled by his coming to town, but he would never have told them why he was going anyway.

The feeling – the urge to move – had been inside him for a long time. He had never understood where it came from, and it frustrated him. He had been content and then, one morning, like a mosquito bite, the need to move agitated him until he couldn't ignore it. And he wanted to see Siena.

The journey took an hour, and the farmworkers sat and dozed on flattened cardboard boxes, blankets, cushions, and jackets. Kriekie stood, listening to two women plotting how to smuggle a papsak past the farmer on the way back. They all knew the old Afrikaner owned a sharp biltong knife which he kept in the bakkie's cubbyhole. It was a knife that came easily into his hands, and which he plunged with unsympathetic regularity into any papsak destined for his farm.

'I have brought string,' said one of the women, taking out a knot of baling twine from a plastic packet. 'I will tie the papsak under my skirt, but then you must be ready to help me up or else it will fall out and he will see I have something. Remember now.'

'You are such a skinny old crow. This boer is going to see straight away that you have a new bum,' said the other, and everyone laughed.

'Julle kan maar lag, but tonight when you feel like a doppie to wash away this dust from your throats it is me you will say thank you to.'

'If this man catches you, then there goes all your pay into the sand,' said one of the men. 'Go drink in the shebeen. Leave the papsak.'

'Nee,' said the woman, 'my oumatjie is longing for a doppie. I promised her I would bring her something from town. And, anyways, dis my reg to have a doppie in my own house.'

'It's not your house – it's the boer's house. And if you are not careful, you are going to find yourself living in your very own backyard hok.' Everyone laughed and Kriekie smiled. He knew by lunchtime, when the farmer headed home, it would be with an empty bakkie. By then, everyone would be drunk and they would be abandoned to find their own way back to the farm. Next week, with sore heads and contrite hearts, they would wait at the kitchen door to beg for their jobs. The farmer, like he always did, would wave his hands and tell them to voetsak, that they were all useless, that he no longer needed them and had made another plan. And then, by the middle of the week, work would start again – as if the weekend had never happened – and everything would go back to normal, until the next time.

Kriekie had been on the farm for a long time. When he reflected on his life, he knew these years were when he had been most at peace. After that night when he'd left Aunt Esme and Seekoegat Primary, he had wandered through the veld for days, watching farmers and their workers fix fences, check water, and set rooikat traps as he lay hidden between the rocks of the koppies above them. This farmer, whom he had chosen, was an older man with a wide pink face shaded by a battered veld hat. He was grumpy and aloof, but he didn't shout, and gave instructions with patience. Kriekie recognised, as he watched from his hiding place, that he had found a steady man.

He hadn't asked for a job, but squatted at the kitchen door before dawn one day with a dead jackal he had snared as it came under a fence into one of the sheep camps. When the farmer had stepped outside, and his dogs had rushed to sniff at the wild limp body, his day had been immediately better. The farmer knew the camp where Kriekie had killed the jackal. He had lost many lambs there.

'There are more, Meneer,' Kriekie had said.

'Ja, I know. Can you deal with them?' The farmer had looked at Kriekie's curled smashed hands.

'Ja, Meneer.'

'Reg so,' the farmer had said.

A year after he'd arrived, Kriekie had been given Old Samson, a boerperd, that he rode to check the far-off fences and his traps. He had never been on a horse before Old Samson, but the farmer had given him a leg up, and he and Old Samson had headed into the veld. The horse was a companion and Kriekie liked him. Most nights, they came back to the farmhouse so he could give Old Samson lucerne, but sometimes they didn't. With time, Old Samson and Kriekie were part of farm life. The farmworkers knew Kriekie seldom spoke, so no one bothered with him.

But even though he felt settled, the memory of Siena swelled in his heart. In the mornings, when he awoke and the smell of the veld was earthy and new, he thought of Siena. When he saw doves pecking at brakbessies, he saw always that they were two, and he thought of Siena. When he noticed the colours of the veld at dusk, he knew Siena would say, 'Joh, maar's mooi.' He wanted to forget her and be alone with Old Samson, but she came into his mind to tickle and tease so that he thought he was going mad. After one long night, when she had tormented him for hours in his dreams, he'd known it was time to go to town and find her. He remembered she was going for matric and, after that, she had spoken of trying for a town job. She wasn't far. He knew that.

Now, as they drove into town, Kriekie felt the bakkie slow for Saturday shoppers criss-crossing the road. The farmer pulled up on the garage forecourt for the farmworkers to climb down where they could head up the road to Pep or OK Foods. Some went across the road to the footpath that led into the lokasie and others loitered, and Kriekie realised they were waiting for the boer to pull away before they headed to the bottle store next door.

Kriekie moved to the back, out of the way of the pushing and shoving. He looked around, studying the faces of the women sitting on the low grey wall with packets of shopping and sacks of flour. When he turned back, he examined the people in the queue at the kiosk and then the petrol attendants.

'En kyk nou daar,' Kriekie said to himself as he waited to get off. There was Siena – just like that. It was that easy to find her. She was filling up a car with petrol and, in that instant, she looked up and into Kriekie's eyes. Neither moved, nor did their faces change. None of the shouting, laughing farmworkers heard Kriekie's intake of breath. No one saw Siena's legs bend slightly. They held each other's gaze until she smiled, a big, teasing, eyes-dancing smile, and he looked away, smiling too but feeling shy. The bakkie was empty, and the farmer waited for Kriekie to get down. He saw him smile and noticed Siena. Kriekie jumped off the bakkie, shaking his head, but the farmer said nothing. Perhaps he knew that the days of Kriekie and Old Samson's riding the boundary fences were done.

Kriekie squatted alongside a tangled hedge, away from the cars and the people, waiting for the forecourt to clear so that Siena would come to him. It was busy and, when she came, it was only for a little while before the next car pulled up.

'Now what wind blew you in?' she said, putting her hands on his face. 'You look well, Kriekie. Sjoe!'

'I have been working,' he said.

'Joh … Are you happy?'

'Yes … Siena?'

'Wag eers – there is another car.'

'Siena?'

'I am coming now-now.'

He sat all morning, watching her fill up cars and bakkies, pump tyres, and carry cooldrink crates into the kiosk. When he saw her restocking the wood pile, he rose to help her.

'Ag dankie, Kriekie. We need to bring out another twenty bundles. And we must count them.'

Afterwards, she gave him a Coke.

'So, what are your plans?' she asked.

'I came to find you.'

She smiled but he saw her shoulders sag.

'Why do you want to find me? You must live your life. My life will make your happy life too complicated.'

The sting was unexpected, and he withdrew to the hedge. Siena followed him, going down on her haunches beside him, taking his hands like she always did. Hers were rough with oil-stained nails, and he smelt petrol and soap on her.

'I have this man, Boetie, living in the hok with us. Wait! He is not my boyfriend, but he thinks he is. I need to deal with this, but I don't know how to. If you come back now, it is going to be difficult for me.' She stood when a car pulled up. The driver waited at the pump, staring at them, and she hurried back to the forecourt. While she was distracted, he rose and walked away.

He remembered Boetie: they had smoked Aunt Esme's cigarette at the sports fields in Oudtshoorn, the one Siena had hugged, and whose hollow tik-face had been all smiles and need. Rage reared and swayed inside him, its venom-filled fangs sinking into his heart. This man had no rights over Siena. Like he had earlier in the day, Kriekie shook his head to clear his vision, but this time the red heat would not go and he stumbled. He crossed to the footpath and, in the lokasie, bought tobacco and a paper twist of dagga from a Somali shop. It was lunchtime, and the people on the street were drunk and troublesome. He made his way towards the outskirts, passing the corrugated hokke on the edge of the veld. In the last yard, he found him, lying on a mattress pulled out onto a square of grass. There were others, on their backs, blowing blue smoke rings into the clear air and dragging on beer quarts. One was busy with a lighter and a tik pipe, and, when he looked up at the passing stranger, Kriekie saw only dead eyes and belligerence. He stopped at the gate.

'Hullo, my broers.' They stared but said nothing.

'I have come from the farm and I am looking for a bietjie geselskap while I smoke my dagga-pil. Can I sit a bit?'

Boetie watched him, his eyes narrow and calculating. 'Kom maar.'

Kriekie opened the gate and crossed the yard so that he could squat under Siena's little tree. He busied himself with a scrap of newspaper, using his crooked little finger to scrape tobacco and dagga into a heap to make his joint. His cigarettes were untidy, but practice had enabled him to make do. Once it was lit, he took a drag and reached over to the nearest man, passing it on. They smoked in silence, and then Boetie said: 'Do I know you?'

'Nee, my broer, I am here in town looking for work. Can you help me?'

'We don't chase sheep,' Boetie said, and the others laughed.

'I can do other things.'

Boetie lay on his side, watching Kriekie. 'With so skeef hands?'

Kriekie looked at his damaged fingers, then turned his hands over, studying his palms. The dagga-pil came back to him and he smoked again.

'Aw'rite … Stick around here and I can give you some work. I got a business going. But you sleep outside. Verstaan?'

Kriekie nodded. 'Okay, I will do your things.'

When the afternoon became cooler, the men moved off. Boetie stayed in the yard, sitting on a chair with his back to the hok, drinking a beer. His eyes were bloodshot and unfocused. 'Go and sit at the back. I don't want you where I can see you,' Boetie said.

Kriekie shifted and stood. His eyes were on the road, watching for Siena. He would have liked to have made a fire, but he said nothing, moving behind the hok, where he sat in the growing dark, listening to the shouting and crying and barking of the lokasie. An owl settled on a street pole and, beyond the noise of people, he heard the bleating, squealing, screeching, and howling of the veld settling at the end of the day. When he took the farmer's biltong knife from his pocket, the night was well in, and in the distance the street lights had come on.

Kriekie dozed, and then heard Siena singing to a child in the hok. She was beside him but on the other side of the corrugated iron. The child, a girl, sang along in places, too, and when they stopped, there was giggling. He lay against the corrugated iron, remembering Seekoegat Primary and the times he had slept on Aunt Esme's roof. It had always been like this, listening from the outside to others sing and laugh, but tonight their voices were beautiful and he felt happy.

In the early hours, Siena woke him again, but she was crying. He sat up, his heart racing, and felt for the knife. There was scuffling, and then her crying again.

'Nee, los my uit … Los my uit …'

There was a long silence, and then the silent sobs of a person weeping into their hands in a corner. The door of the hok opened and, when Kriekie crawled to the edge, he saw the shape of a man leaving. He was glad he was back and, as the disturbed air settled again, he understood what had pulled him to town.

Chapter 19

NOW

Siena sat under the afdak outside the kitchen at Seekoegat Primary, eyes closed and head resting on the support pillar. Her hands were one on top of the other in her lap, and her bare feet, with their scabbed and stubbed toes and broken nails, were crossed at the ankles. The ground was cool, the shadow from the prefabricated building behind her still long as the morning sun uncurled and stretched on the horizon turning the veld orange. The heat would build, but this was the time of day when Karoo people opened doors and windows to let in the air.

The boys, who yesterday had been playing in the dry river, were on her mind. Aunt Esme had said they were gone, but Siena thought she should find them today and ask their people to leave them at Seekoegat Primary. They should come for grade one, she thought. It was a waste for children not to come for grade one when it could be done so close to where they lived. If they were off a karretjie, their people could leave them here. She must find them and explain that she had once been off a karretjie too, but that this school had been good to her and there was food here. There was no need to make fires to cook tortoises because they were starving. If Pa were alive, he could have tracked them and spoken to them. He would have known their people, like he did all the karretjie people in the Karoo, and they would have listened.

'People who live on donkey carts are our family,' he said. 'We are the ones who come from the beginning. We were here when the springbok crossed the plains with the eland and the gemsbok in great herds and there were no fences or towns.' If this was true, Siena thought now, those boys were her brothers.

Siena had awoken in Aunt Esme's bed with the grey dawn reaching in through the open window. Ma and Sussie were in the bed with her and, as she stirred, she'd felt the touching of familiar bodies.

'Wake up, Siena, you are sleeping too much.' Sussie's child voice and her fingers trying to prize open her eyelids had eased a pressure within her.

'Los haar uit.' It was Ma.

She had turned over and buried her face in the pillow, enjoying the feeling of Sussie, moving on and off the mattress, bouncing to wake her up. Aunt Esme was up, feeding her chickens … *kiep-kiep* … *kiep-kiep* … and the old dog whined, flapping his ears and rattling his chain.

'Mamma?' Siena's voice had croaked.

'Siena?'

'Mamma and Sussie …' She'd smiled and looked at them. 'Is jy okay?'

'Ma …' She'd reached over and taken Ma's hand.

'We thought you were dead.'

'Nee, Sussie!'

Sussie had climbed over her and pushed her legs under the blanket, so she was between Siena and the wall. 'Are you better? Can you get up?'

'Sussie, moenie nou so lastig wees 'ie,' Ma had grumbled.

'It's okay, Ma.' Siena had pushed herself up, putting her

174

arm around Sussie and pulling her close. The child wriggled down and rested her head on Siena's lap, her thumb in her mouth. There were just the chickens clucking and Sussie's sucking.

'Ma, what have I done?'

Ma had shifted off the bed and onto the ground, moving on her haunches to the corner near the door, where she'd rolled a cigarette from newspaper, lit a match and, lifting her chin, inhaled hard so the tobacco took. Sussie was asleep, and Siena stroked her cheek and throat.

'I am happy he is dead.'

'Nee, Ma.'

'He turned our life upside down.'

'Oh, Ma … but it is terrible what I have done.'

Siena had closed her eyes, and Boetie's man-face, with his blood-flecked eyes and thin scabbed lips, came at her so that she flinched and murmured and Sussie lifted her head and looked up.

'Dis okay, Sussie, ssshhh.'

When he had come back from Oudtshoorn after all those years, Siena had thought it would be like before, when they were in the valley. She had thought she could handle his nonsense; the sadness and the anger of the left-behind boy.

The mevrou should have brought him to Seekoegat too. Meneer Maans would have sorted him out, but Pa had wanted him gone. What was his life worth in the end? Siena wiped her face with the corner of the blanket. Every night in the hok, with the drinking and the dagga smoking and then the tik, it was the same. 'Los my, los my …'

When Boetie would leave to go who-knows-where into the dark, Siena would creep outside to fill the bucket at the aunt's tap and wash herself. Sometimes, he would come back, and she would wake up with men in the hok drinking beer and smoking. Through it all, she had been too ashamed to tell the aunt next door or the women at church.

Aunt Esme's bed creaked as Siena lifted Sussie onto the pillow and swung her legs to the floor. She should wash; the police would be here soon.

'Have the police been, Ma?'

'No one is here, just the old lady. The meneer has gone to Oudtshoorn. The school is closed for holidays.'

Aunt Esme's voice came across the yard and Sussie sat up. 'Where are my people? Is ou Klimmie awake? Opstaan, opstaan. Breakfast is ready.'

On the kitchen stoep, Siena sat in her old spot where she could look out over the veld, and Aunt Esme gave her coffee in the same mug from long ago.

'See, my ou Klimmie, I have never forgotten you. Isn't the morning too beautiful?'

She remembered Boetie had come back early and she knew he had been busy with tik. He had wanted wine and to kiss her. Sussie had been there and, when Siena saw how he was, she told her to go next door and sleep at the aunt.

'No. She stays here.' He had been on his feet, the lovey-dovey person from a minute before gone.

'Sit on the floor.' He'd pointed for Sussie to go into a corner.

'Boetie, she is going to the aunt.'

'Sit on the floor.'

'Boetie ... asseblief.'

Those little boys in the riverbed had been the same age as Sussie. They should all be in grade one and play together. Maybe one day they would make it to matric and they could have good jobs and live in houses and eat shop food and not be pulled this way and that across the veld or live in hokke on the edge of the lokasie.

It was when he'd touched Sussie that Siena had picked up the broken beer bottle. *Do what you like to me, but do not touch this little girl.* The memory of the stew mixed with beer and then the hot metal stink of his blood made her vomit, and she turned and retched off the stoep.

Her Boetie.

The boy whose smile she had loved and thought about so many times was dead. Her friend. In the end, he had terrified her.

'Klimmie?'

'It's okay. I'm okay.'

Aunt Esme was next to her, wiping her face with a wet lappie and Sussie, who had been playing in the sand, was on her feet, taking her hands. Ma, still on her haunches smoking in the shade, watched.

'One day at a time, Klimmie. Slowly, slowly.'

'Aunt, must I write down what happened? For the police? Do they want that?'

A brown butterfly rested on a red geranium that Aunt Esme had planted at the gate leading into the yard. The soil around the plant had been pushed up to make a dam which was stained dark from a recent watering.

'It's the only way to have something pretty in this place,' Aunt Esme had said. 'Someone has to give them water.'

'Can you give me a paper and a pencil?'

'Drink your coffee, Klimmie. Don't worry about police stories now. There are no police here.'

Siena leant back and breathed to control her shaking. She noticed for the first time that she was wearing different clothes and her bloodied clothes were gone. She could smell these clothes had been washed with green Sunlight soap.

'Kyk hier, Siena, kyk hier.' Sussie drew in the sand with a stick.

'You must write your name,' Siena said. 'Do you remember how I showed you?'

'Ssss, like a snake ... Sssussie and also Ssssiena.'

'You are so clever. You will go all the way to matric.' She leant against the pillar and wiped her mouth again with the lappie.

The sun rose higher and Ma shifted. Siena looked over at her but neither spoke. The older woman swatted at a fly and turned to look out over the veld. Siena knew it wouldn't be long now and she would agitate to go back to town for a drink.

'Sussie, who fetched you and Ma here?'

'The school meneer. He said you were tired and we must come with him to Seekoegat so that we can make you open your eyes.'

'Sus ... what happened when I ran away ... That ... man ...?'

Sussie drew in the sand and then looked up at Siena. 'Die ou is dood, Siena.'

'I know.'

'I fetched the next-door aunt and we came back to our hok. You had run away but there was another ou there.'

'One of his tjommies?'

'No, it was one I didn't know. He had a knife and he was also cutting the ou's throat some more. Like he wanted to make sure he was properly dead. The aunt was screaming and I saw there was blood all over him. The ou looked at me and said, "Nou is hy dood. When the police come, tell them it was me." Then he ran away too. There was blood on our new table and on the ground. He was on the ground and his eyes were like this.' Sussie stopped talking and opened her eyes wide. 'The aunt was shouting all the time: "He is dead, he is dead."'

Aunt Esme stood in the kitchen doorway, listening. Ma

picked up her mug from between her feet and held it with both hands, her eyes moving from Sussie to Siena.

Sussie, unused to being allowed to talk, carried on. 'Then the aunt shouted: "Siena, where is Siena? What has this rubbish man done with Siena?" I told the aunt, "Don't worry, Siena ran away," but she was shouting so much that she didn't listen.'

'Sussie … did the police come?'

'Ja, the police came but I ran into the veld and I hid away. When it was getting light, Mamma found me there and we climbed up the koppie to the big rocks. I don't know if the police caught that strange ou. I didn't see him again but I didn't tell anyone anything after that. Nobody asked me. The aunt was shouting all the time, "These rubbish men have taken my Siena."'

Siena stood and walked past the red geraniums, where the butterfly was still moving from flower to flower and out the gate. She crossed the gravel, where the bus had once waited to take them to Oudtshoorn for athletics, and stopped where the veld started. The plains were dry but so beautiful. If she could, she would stay at Seekoegat Primary forever. It was strange how here, even though there was nothing – just the school – her soul was at peace. This was where she felt safe, where life was the same.

A tread in the gravel made her turn.

'Aunt Esme?'

Kriekie was behind her and, when he saw he had given her a fright, he covered his face with his arms.

They were both laughing. 'You devil! Have you been here the whole time?'

'Ja, I was here. The aunt told me you needed to sleep and eat. She said that I had made myself scarce for so many years, I could do it for another day.'

When had she last seen him? It was that afternoon at the garage when he'd come off that farm bakkie and she had told him Boetie was staying with her.

'I followed you here from town,' he said.

'Now? When I was running from the police? Were you on the Sand River road too?'

'Yes.'

'I killed him, Kriekie.'

She turned away and looked over the veld again, and he came to her side.

The heat made the air shimmer and the cicadas had started their relentless chirruping.

'You know it's kriekies that make that noise? I don't know why you are Kriekie, because you make no noise at all.'

'My ma said it was because I jumped like a kriekie into her arms.'

Siena smiled at the image of Kriekie running towards a mother with open arms. *That's why he was brought here*, she thought, *something happened to the woman who had given him that name.*

'Kriekie, did you see those boys in the river?'

'No. There were no boys, just you, under a bush, holding on to an old tortoise that was hiding in its big shell. That tortoise wanted to go, but your body was curled right around it, like you were protecting it.' He laughed, embarrassed. 'I thought you were dead, Siena. I thought I left you too long. We were so close to Seekoegat when you went into the riverbed and lay down. I didn't think you would give up then. When I saw how you were, I came here and fetched the aunt and the meneer.'

Siena turned back to the veld and, for a while, neither spoke.

'There are a lot of tortoises in this veld,' she said, 'but it is those very big ones who are the most precious. They are as old as the Karoo. They have been here forever.'

'Ja, a tortoise is a beautiful thing,' Kriekie said.

'Those boys in the river were going to eat that big tortoise, but I stopped them even though they were starving. They were very young and I don't know where their people were. But now I am worried that, because they didn't eat the tortoise … because I stopped them … they will die. A child's life is worth much more than a tortoise. They should be in school here; Aunt Esme would feed them.'

Kriekie shook his head but said nothing.

'Ag, my ou Kriekie. There has been so much sadness, nè?'

Aunt Esme was on the stoep and, when she saw them walking back together, she called Sussie and Ma to the kitchen. When Siena and Kriekie came in, Ma was spooning vetkoek batter into a pot of bubbling oil on the stove and Sussie's mouth was full.

'Come sit now,' Aunt Esme said. 'Klimmie, your ma is making her people vetkoek and I have pinched some of the meneer's apricot jam. You and Sussie are safe, and Kriekie has come home to his Aunt Esme. We must be happy and make a little party here. What do you think? Hey, my ou Klimmie.'

Ma turned from the stove with the bowl of hot vetkoek, and looked at Siena and Sussie, who had moved to her lap. Kriekie fetched tin plates from the shelf, and Aunt Esme stirred more coffee and sugar into their mugs.

When Meneer Maans came back with his car, Siena thought, she would ask him to take her back to town to speak to the police. She could not hide from what she had done to Boetie. Ma would go back too, she knew that. But Sussie must stay with Aunt Esme for school.

For now, she would stay too in this place that had saved

her. Seekoegat Primary was, after all, as it always had been – a little school in the Karoo veld, somewhere on the tar road to Beaufort West.